I0686880

CONTENTS

DECEMBER SCANDAL

SCANDALOUS SIBLINGS SERIES
BOOK 3

SUZI LOVE

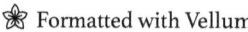 Formatted with Vellum

DECEMBER SCANDAL

In this novella length, stand-alone story, the Jamison family joins the Duke of Sherwyn and the St. Martin clan at the duke's country estate, but the guest numbers double when stranded travelers seek refuge after early December snowfalls make roads impassable.

Michael Brandon travels to introduce Melissa and her daughter to his family, but a missing bridge delays their journey. To their shock, horror, and yet profound relief, Michael's missing brother is carried into the house by the men who rescued him from captivity.

Frederick battles to stay alive long enough to convict his kidnappers and warn his family of danger. But will Michael walk away when he learns the truth?

DEDICATION

To my growing family, this one is for you.
Thanks for your love and support, and especially for allowing me the joy of having grandchildren.

I'm truly grateful.

Suzi Love

To be first to get news about giveaways, new releases, and contests, join my newsletter at www.suzilove.com
And my Facebook Group - Suzi Love's Lovelies

1

1844 Martin House, England.

Michael Brandon strolled after Cayle St. Martin, the Duke of Sherwyn, when the duke strode to the hallway to greet the latest group of travelers. They'd be, like him, grateful to accept the duke's hospitality because they'd all become stranded after heavy snowfalls had led to rapidly rising water levels and an impassable local bridge.

He leaned on a wall and watched Mason, the efficient butler at Martin House, ease open the massive front door while three footmen braced their shoulders against the door to stop it blowing fully open. The house had already been full of family members gathered for Christmas, but with the addition of several groups of half-frozen travelers arriving every hour during the afternoon, the house's walls must be groaning under the excess number of guests needing beds.

Several massive rooms in Martin House had been opened and warmed for the weary travelers who had descended on the duke and his family, but those large fires needed constant feeding with logs of wood. Therefore, Sherwyn couldn't risk a barrage of snow and sleet blowing inside his house from the courtyard because, in such inclement weather, his footmen might not be able to collect more firewood for another week. Little wonder then that the duke hovered near the front entrance and supervised each subsequent arrival, his charming duchess by his side to add her won welcome.

Michael and his party had been the first to beg assistance from Sherwyn this afternoon, as he'd known that Sherwyn had left London a week earlier and would already be in residence at his country home. There had been a flurry of social events in London over the past two weeks before the Ton left the city and retreated to their country estates to wait out the colder months. Though this extreme weather had caught everyone by surprise.

It was barely mid December and the nearby bridge usually served the locals well through that month and into the New Year. Water levels normally only rose and covered the bridge after the snow-storms of January. Michael and Cayle were long time friends and so he knew Cayle had loathed this house, his family seat, when his father and stepmother had been in residence, but now that Cayle was the duke, and a married man, he had decided to turn this house into a more welcoming family gathering place. Even with the influx of visitors, invited or not, the staff here were jolly and efficient, a rare combination in the serving ranks.

The jolliness came from Becca's side of the family. The Jamison's collected staff that were more like stray dogs that no other household would allow across the doorstep. Ex-criminals mostly. Housebreak-ers, street thieves, and several reformed trollops now ran Cayle's houses, and those of his cousin, Richard. A week of extra guests to feed and bed wouldn't stretch Sherwyn's supplies, or their staff, too much, but if this large group remained any longer than a few days, the meals were bound to be less generous than the St Martin and Jamison families expected when they gathered for their Christmas weeks at Martin House.

Michael would feel guilty for landing, unannounced, on the St. Martin's doorstep, with Melissa and her daughter and their retinue in tow, except that he knew he was providing Becca and her sisters with the drama and excitement that they thrived on. The Jamisons had proved their resourcefulness when Becca and her siblings, with help from Cayle and Richard St. Martin, had tracked down a stock-investing madman or, as it had turned out to be, a madwoman, and handed her over to Scotland Yard. Becca, and the other ladies, appeared delighted to have new people and conversations to keep them entertained while snowstorms kept them all housebound.

The children, Richard's nieces and nephews, thought the duke and duchess had especially invited extra playmates to enliven their raucous games, which they played all day at top speed through every hallway and room in the house. Voices echoed from every wing of the grand house as maids scuttled to and fro and put warmed bricks into the newly aired beds in rooms that normally sat unused. Michael had never seen Martin House so busy, or so full of gaiety. And soon both Becca and her sister, Laura, would be adding their babies to the organized chaos.

Michael felt a pang of jealousy for his old friends, Cayle and Richard. He'd known them at school and when he'd returned to London from the continent, he'd been surprised and delighted to discover that the two men, plus Cayle's younger brothers, were all avid investors. And that Becca, with her gift for mathematics, would far rather discuss finances and share her insights and predictions for future stock trading than sit in a drawing room and drink tea with the more upright ladies of the *Ton*. These extra avenues of steady income made Michael confident that he could support a wife, namely Melissa, if she'd have him. And he already adored her energetic daughter, Freda.

Truth be told, this was the first time he'd seen Cayle look comfortable in his role of lord of the manor and the highest-ranking peer in the county, or seen this previously cold mansion as a warm and welcoming home. As boys home from school for the traditional Christmas celebrations, Cayle and his two younger brothers had felt ill at ease here, especially after their father remarried and their scheming stepmother had made it clear that she disliked interrupting her busy London social life to bored in the country for two weeks in December. Having three boys in residence, plus visiting boys such as Michael, had eaten into her time playing hostess to her toad-eating friends from London, most of whom had only been dragged to the country by the lure of free room and board and a way to avoid London's frozen and dangerous streets.

Cayle was the sort of man who'd have opened his home to these strangers even if the vicar hadn't sent a request to open the extra rooms at Martin House. All day they'd opened the door to welcome weary, and sometimes frightened, people who'd been trapped in carriages and coaches on the snow laden roads and before the weather closed in fully, Cayle had sent two footmen out to check the roads near his house and bring the stranded inside, no matter their rank or social class. The Jamison sisters had, as per usual, predicted the day's dramas and had the staff cleaning and cooking long before the first stranded group arrived at their door.

Michael had given up trying to understand how the Jamison family arrived at their insights or made such accurate predictions. Cayle laughed at Michael's puzzlement and would simply shrug. 'The five siblings,' he'd say, 'have more intelligence in their little fingers than the entire House of Lords have in their collective heads.' Richard, Laura's husband and cousin to Cayle advised to simply accept the mystery of them and enjoy the bountiful results. Laura was a herbalist and perfumer whose extraordinary sense of smell carried over into reading the personal traits and emotions of everyone she met. She and Richard had recently returned from their honeymoon trip to Europe and Laura was so excited about returning from Paris *enceinte*, as the French would say, grabbed the hand of anyone near her and press it to her rounded abdomen, much to the chagrin of her aunt who repeatedly apologized for her niece's lack of manners. Richard, the father to be, merely stood by and grinned, obviously entertained rather than embarrassed by his countess's gauche display of joy at carrying their baby.

Charlotte, the most stunningly beautiful debutante London had ever seen, smiled serenely at each influx of guests. Well known to be the calmest and most ladylike of the Jamison sisters, she was nevertheless a radical in her won way. Her obsession with the new science of Phrenology was driving her siblings mad because she insisted on reading their head bumps and then trying to explain how it showed their personal traits. Michael chuckled. At least Charlotte now had an influx of new subjects, and new heads, on whom to test her new-found skills. Unfortunately for Brian, Cayle's brother, he would no longer be Charlotte's only willing subject. During a conversation at their club, Cayle had revealed that the family had expected Brian's infatuation with the delectable Charlotte to have dwindled by now, but Brian still followed the poor girl around like an over zealous puppy. Charlotte was the epitome of kindness and would never speak unkindly to another person, unlike Becca whose unladylike language could blister the hide off anyone who dared cross her, or a member of her family.

Becca, Cayle's redheaded and fiery tempered duchess, walked to Cayle's side, pushing her hip into his in that comfortable way she had of leaning into her husband and blending their bodies, in the same ways their minds so often agreed. Cayle slid his arm around his wife's back and rubbed in gentle circles, knowing Becca leaned her weight onto him because their growing babe was stretching her petite size to the limit and putting excess pressure on her back. Though the duchess was so stubborn that she'd never rest in her room while there was work to be done. Poor Cayle despaired of ever getting her to slow down, so he massaged her aches and encouraged her to sit instead of standing. A well-trained footman slid a chair under Becca's knees from behind, giving her no choice but to sit.

From beside her, Michael heard her whisper to Cayle, "You've told them to do that every time I'm on my feet, haven't you?"

"Someone has to be sensible during this pregnancy," Cayle muttered. "Or our daughter will arrive before her time and create even more havoc in our lives."

"I expect that our *son*," Becca said, "will arrive whenever *he* decides, because he's certain to be like every other man in the St. Martin family and march to his own beat."

From the other side of Becca's chair, Laura and Charlotte joined Michael in laughing at the contrary pair.

"Exactly," Laura said, beaming up at Richard, who'd joined the welcoming party.

Richard smiled serenely. "Ah, my darling wife, we may be unpredictable, but you enjoyed my new game of pirate captain and captured maiden last night, didn't you?" He waggled his eyebrows suggestively, causing Becca and Charlotte to titter.

Michael couldn't help but laugh. "Good Lord, Laura," he said. "I had no idea that you could blush."

Laura reached across Becca and gave him a friendly punch on the arm.

Cayle grinned at Richard. "Whatever game you played did last night, cousin, must have been adventurous, because you've made our brazen Laura blush." He looked at Charlotte. "You're supposedly the innocent Jamison sister, so why aren't you scandalized by the notion of your sister being chased around her bedroom by a pirate?"

"Becca and Laura taught me everything they know long ago, my dear brother-in-law. Little shocks me now."

They all gasped as a strong gust of wind blew down the hallway. Several well-bundled figures were hurried around the door and into the house by Mason. The footmen pushed hard, slamming the front door closed behind them, while melting snow made puddles on the marble floor at the feet of the newcomers. The gathered family shivered at the burst of frigid air, but resolutely stayed to greet the newest arrivals, who were being helped with their outer garments by Mason and his staff.

Michael watched Becca stand and lace her arm through Cayle's, accepting his support but too stubborn to retreat until she'd identified who had arrived and organized where they needed be housed and fed. A little girl's squeals echoed as Freda, the daughter of Melissa Brandon, a widow and the lady Michael hoped to soon wed, raced into the hallway from the back parlor. Two small boys, the sons of one of Richard's sisters, were hot on her heels, yelling for her to come back and let the pirates tie their captive to the ship's mast. Freda squealed again, a high-pitched sound that should grate on everyone's ears but them all laugh instead, and ran full tilt towards Laura and hid herself in Laura's skirts. Her mother hurried into the hallway, huffing and puffing, and obviously embarrassed at her daughter's excitement over the game and being chased by two boys.

"Freda's starting early," Richard said with a grin. He looked down to where her impish face peeped out from the folds of his wife dress. "Most girls are at least eleven before they learn what fun it is to have all the boys run after you."

Freda giggled and smiled up at Richard, while she swung on Laura's skirt. "Will you catch me?"

"Ah, yes," Laura said drolly to her husband, patting his arm. "Clearly another female infatuated by your dimples, my love."

Just as Freda stepped out of Laura's skirt and into Richard's arms, Melissa skidded to a halt in front of them. A few wisps of hair had escaped from the knot at the back of her neck and her face was red. Michael moved to Melissa's side and took her arm, patting her hand soothingly.

"She's too fast for me these days," Melissa said, struggling for breath. She looked at Cayle and Becca. "I apologize for Freda disturbing you when you are greeting new..." Her words trailed away, worrying Michael.

"Are you all right, Mrs. Brandon," Michael asked, being careful to address Melissa formally in front of these strangers.

In private, he called her far more intimate names, and he ached for time alone with her so he could whisper those pet names into her ear and watch her eyes go wide with excitement. He loved hearing her breath catch with anticipation when he explained all the ways he would touch her, later, when they were alone.

His original plan had been to propose to Melissa on Christmas Eve and arrange a small wedding in the local church as early as possible in the New Year. But delays on their trip had made him impatient. He wanted the right to claim Melissa publicly as his wife, and to have her in his bed every night, without her fretting about them causing a scandal by being caught *en flagrante*.

But Melissa didn't answer his concerned enquiry. She stood as still as a garden statue, staring, open-mouthed, at the man who'd been carried inside on an invalid's chair. One of his attendants had

pulled back the blanket and removed his scarf, exposing part of the
man's face. Sunken eyes and a gaunt face indicated that the haggard-
looking man had recently lost a lot of flesh. His mouth was pinched
and his lips were blue from cold and the obvious pain he suffered.

As Sherwyn stepped forward towards the man, Melissa gave an
unladylike squeal, her knees buckled, and she clasped her arms
around her body and rocked back and forth. Michael rushed to slide
his arm around her waist, but she slumped downwards until he could
barely keep her upright. If she fainted, she'd hit her head on the
marble floor and do untold damage. He growled, and Richard rushed
to Melissa's other side and slipped his shoulder under her arm and
helped keep her upright.

Quick-witted Laura grabbed the chair that Becca had been using
and slid it beneath Melissa, easing it behind her knees. Together, he
and Richard eased her onto the chair, but Michael didn't dare let her
go for fear she'd slump forwards and topple out of the chair.

Melissa's face was ghostly pale and he felt the tremors running
through her body, yet her entire focus was on the frail figure in the
invalid chair. Her eyes closed and her body slid, lifeless, down the
chair and towards the floor. He hauled her upright again, while
Richard pushed a footstool in front of the chair and Laura lifted
Melissa's feet onto the embroidered top.

What the hell was going on? The Melissa he knew was strong and
lively, and certainly not given to fainting spells. He crouched beside
her chair, keeping his forearm across her waist to hold her in place.
Across from him, Laura patted Melissa's hand and spoke soft words of
reassurance to her until Melissa moaned and stirred. He moaned
with relief, not caring what onlookers might see or hear. Hiding the
depth of his feelings for Melissa had been hard enough in London,
where he'd been determined that the gossips would see nothing of
impropriety regarding his relationship with Melissa, a widow and
mother. But her, now, with her looking as white as a corpse, he didn't
give a damn what they thought. He simply needed her to wake up, to
speak to him, so he could breathe freely again.

When Melissa's eyelids fluttered open, he heaved a sigh of relief and lifted her hand to his lips for a kiss. Mason offered her a glass of water, but her hands shook so much when she held it that water splashed onto her bodice and Michael wrapped his hands over hers to help lift the glass to her mouth. Melissa, normally so careful about her appearance, and Freda's, didn't notice the wet splotches on her bodice or her shaking hands. Her gaze was fixed, unblinkingly, on the blanket wrapped man.

Michael urged her to take some more sips of water, his clenched muscles relaxing fractionally when the liquid revived his love a little and her cheeks took on a pinkish flush. He handed the glass to Mason and stood, keeping his hand on Melissa's arm as he turned to peer at the man who'd caused Melissa's violent reaction.

"Oh, my God," Michael yelled, as he felt the color drain from his own face. He reached out to grip the top of the wooden chair, steadying himself so that he wouldn't follow Melissa's example and slide towards the floor in a faint.

Bent at the waist, hands on his knees, Michael dragged in one ragged breath after another and waited for his body to recover from the shock of his discovery. He willed the spinning in his head to slow, forced himself to draw long slow breaths, and finally stood erect. At some point, Cayle and Richard had moved to his side, ready to rescue him before he also succumbed to a ungentlemanly-like faint. After several agonizing moments, his knees stopped knocking and he could stand erect.

He took three steps towards the man and shook his head. "They said you were dead." His hand fluttered towards the man in the invalid chair, whose eyes had slowly opened and his hands twitched in his lap. "We'd given up hope of ever seeing you again," Michael murmured. "Every investigator eventually told us the same thing. Each year, the chances of you still being alive diminished, and if you lived, they would have found some trace of you by now."

Shocked gasps came from several of the bystanders, as they understood the significance of his words. Michael, Sherwyn, and Richard mixed in the same level of London society and were members of the same clubs, so the men knew of his long quest to find

Frederick, or his body, and bring him home. Obviously Becca and Laura and the others also now recognized the identity of their most recent unexpected guest. The servants stepped aside and stood at attention along the wall, the man's attendants removed the remainder of his outdoor clothing, and Michael had a clear view of the frail looking man's shape, size, and face. He swallowed hard, barely able to speak. "Is it truly you, Frederick?"

Behind him, Melissa was crying, heart breaking sobs that escalated in volume and uncontained emotions. Unable to think about her distress for the moment, Michael took another step forward. A second step brought him closer to the chair and the white-haired man who resembled Frederick, and yet appeared too old and too fragile to be the man who'd suddenly disappeared three years ago. He reached out, his hand trembling harder than Melissa's had when she'd held the glass to her lips. One of the men who'd carried the chair inside moved forwards and held out his hand to Michael, but he was engrossed in his survey of the lined and scarred face before him to observe the formalities.

An older man with military bearing spoke, finally drawing Michael's eyes away from the ill man, a man whose features used to be as familiar to Michael as his own in the mirror and yet now seemed more like a stranger's.

"Yes," the older man said, "this man is Lord Brandon. Frederick Brandon, formally of Upper Laidstowe. Are you related to him?"

Michael couldn't find the words to answer. His gaze swung back to this new and widely different Frederick, searching for clues to convince him that this thin stranger was the man he'd always called brother.

Finally, he nodded. "Yes, I'm related to Lord Brandon, Frederick, who disappeared four years ago." He faced the sick man and spoke directly to him. "We searched everywhere for you. Men scoured the streets of London for weeks after you disappeared, and then we widened our search. Ports, inns, the countryside, anywhere you might have gone. Or anywhere that you might have been taken if you'd been kidnapped and held for ransom."

Michael groaned. "Three years of nothing. Not a sign. The police declared you a missing person, most likely deceased, and told us to wait out the seven years until we could officially declare you dead." He swiped at his eyes, brushing aside the gathering tears. He took Frederick's hand. "But we never gave up hope. None of us, and especially not mother."

Tears trickled down Michael's cheek and he brushed them aside impatiently. He didn't care that everyone saw his raw grief. He only cared that his brother, if this shell of a man truly was his previously vibrant brother, heard his words and understood the truth in them. The heartache and sorrow that they'd all carried for years. The pain they'd suffered thinking they might never set eyes on Frederick again.

"Your mother ..." His words caught as a sob escaped him, echoing the continuing sobbing from Melissa behind him. "Your mother died a year ago, but her last words were a desperate plea for me to keep looking for you. To find you, and to bring you home."

Michael watched tears trickle and run over the creases on the aged face before him, and he knew. This was Frederick, his constant companion during hundreds of childish escapades.

"You're freezing." He used his thumb to wipe away Frederick's tears. "Let's shift you to a warm fire before we talk any more."

Frederick looked like he wanted to speak but was too weak to form any words. He gave a small nod before his eyes closed.

Two of Sherwyn's footmen carried the chair into the drawing room while one of Frederick's attendants hovered beside them. One man remained in the hallway with them and he walked to Michael and held out his hand.

"My name is Hendrix. Joseph Hendrix. I worked at the naval office for many years, but now I simply help out when they have a special request."

"And I'm Michael Brandon, one of Frederick's only surviving family members." He shook the man's hand, holding longer than was polite. "Thank you for bringing Frederick home."

"My name is Hendrix. Joseph Hendrix. I worked at the naval office for many years, but now I simply help out when they have a special request. I was traveling to my own home near here anyway, so when someone requested that I accompany poor Lord Brandon and assist the men that our government hired to care for him, I was more than happy to agree. During his voyage home, his lordship shared a lot of information with the ship's captain, who carefully wrote it all down and handed Frederick's reports into the naval office as soon as they arrived on British soil. We now have first-hand information on the locations of several pirate ships and their crews. Plus, several key pieces to help solve puzzles that have troubled the government for several years about how the pirates always knew where, and when, our navy would sail. Britain's ships are now in a far better position to track down, and arrest, the rebel captains who have continually attacked our ships. Ensuring that Frederick arrived at his final destination and was able to speak with his family was the least the government could do to assist him."

He gave a small smile and shrugged. "But with the bridge out, we ended up here instead." He gave Sherwyn a nod of acknowledgement. "We are very grateful for your hospitality, Your Grace, as Lord Brandon was suffering dreadfully with the cold." He looked at Michael. "Quite a coincidence meeting someone from Lord Brandon's family here, today." He sighed. "His Lordship's story is long and complicated." He glanced at the gathered ladies listening intently to the conversation. "And some of the things he endured are rather horrifying, and not fitting for the ears of ladies."

Becca stepped forward and offered her hand to Hendrix. "I think you'll find that these ladies know more than you imagine about the seedier side of life, and that we're not easily shocked." She took his arm and led him towards the drawing room." But please, come and be comfortable first. Then we can hear Lord Brandon's story."

After Becca drew the group down the hallway, Richard carrying a giggling Freda in his arms, Michael turned back to Melissa. She'd remained seated in the background. Her face was as white as a wash day sheet, her eyes large, and she looked as shocked as he'd been when he thought he was seeing a ghost. He frowned.

Perhaps Melissa had seen a ghost from her past. He'd never

considered that she might have known Frederick, but it seemed likely as her parent's estate was quite near to where his family lived. Because he'd spent so many years away from England, Michael had lost track of which local families the Brandons had socialized with over the years. His aunt, really his substitute mother, had been a diligent letter writer, but her rambling snippets of news were never in chronological order and her missives had been weeks, or months, old when he'd received them.

Consequently, he'd often not bothered piecing together of whom she'd spoken, where they'd lived, and when she'd seen them. Also, he'd not been in England when Frederick had disappeared. He'd returned home as quickly as possible when he'd been informed that Frederick had gone missing, possibly taken by force, and had thrown himself into the search. Nothing had mattered except finding the man who'd been his constant companion all his life, his best friend, to his home, and relieving the distress his family had suffered since one of their clan had been proclaimed missing, presumed dead.

Michael crouched before Melissa and took her hands in his, rubbing them absently to warm her cold fingers. It was an instinctive action and one he'd done a dozen times before Melissa was often without her gloves, even out in public. In places like the park, Melissa said it was easier to play with her daughter, to wash her three-year-old face, and to soothe her little girl's hurts without gloves.

Scenarios of when Frederick and Melissa might have met ran through his head. Her shock at seeing his brother's face was as genuine as his own had been, yet Melissa had appeared more than simply surprised to see Frederick. She'd looked horrified, frantic, and devastated, all at the same time.

"Melissa, you knew Frederick before today?" She stared at him in horror and then looked away. "At our family home? Or yours? Or perhaps in London?"

She swallowed, sighed, and met his eyes again. She gave a quick nod. "I met your brother at a local assembly a few years ago and then, later, we attended many of the same events in London."

"Why didn't you tell me knew him? I told you he was missing. Told you of how we still searched for him."

She swiped at the tears wetting her cheeks. She stared at a point over his shoulder as if trying to clear her thoughts, and not meeting his gaze.

"I'm so sorry, Michael. I should have told you the truth long before this, but there never seemed to be a right time. I've been so happy the past few months that I was too cowardly to ruin our friendship before I'd had a bit more time with you." Her breath hitched on another sob and she bowed her head. Putting his fingers gently under her chin, he lifted her face to meet his eyes again.

"I can't imagine you being cowardly about anything. You're such a strong person." He fleetingly touched his lips to hers. "You've lost a husband and raised a daughter. People admire you, Melissa, more than you realize. I certainly do."

She gave a long mournful groan and sprang to her feet. She pushed him away and started towards the door. "No, you don't understand. I'm weak and cowardly and no one will admire me when they hear what I've done." Another loud sob escaped and she put a hand to her mouth, trying to smother the anguished noises she was making. "I've told lies. People will hate me." She cried into her handkerchief as she hurried towards the staircase. "You'll hate me." She gave a loud wail that echoed around the high-ceilinged hall, picked up her skirts, and ran to the bottom of the carpeted steps.

He hurried after her, and as she started to race up the steps, he said, "I could never hate you, my love. Never."

2

*M*elissa reached her room, out of breath, and unable to stop crying. She'd ducked her head whenever she met a servant in the hallway, knowing her strange behavior would be discussed at length in the kitchens, yet too distraught to face the servants with her tear ravaged face, or to let them see how close she was to screaming out loud. She locked her door and curled up in a ball on the bed, her body racked by uncontrollable sobs.

Frederick was alive. Frederick was here, downstairs in this very house, and most likely revealing every detail of his disappearance and explaining his reappearance. She groaned. She needed to be there to hear what he'd tell them all, but if she'd sat with the others in the drawing room and listened to his story, she'd have been in Frederick's sight. Would he recognize her? Had he already seen her face and remembered her?

He might well have blurted out the story of their relationship in front of these kind and generous people, men and women that she'd hoped would become her friends. God knew she'd had few enough friends after her many years of exile from her parent's home. When Michael had introduced her to the St. Martin men, and to the

Jamison siblings, she'd been thrilled. Overcome that they'd gathered her into their fold simply because she was a friend of Michael's.

Friend. She was much more than that, or at least she had been until forty minutes ago. Was Frederick telling Michael of their past relationship at this very moment? More importantly, what was she going to tell Michael? She'd stupidly thought she'd have time to explain it to him, in private, and before they announced anything to Michael's family. She'd foolishly allowed herself to dream again, and now every joyous thought she'd had for her future, and for Freda's, was about to be destroyed.

Her father had repeatedly warned her that one day her past sins would come back to haunt her, and now the unveiling of her sinful past would have even more dire consequences than either she, or her unforgiving father, could ever have imagined. She'd been forced to leave her home on the very day she'd discovered that she was carrying a baby. Thankfully, her mother had come to stay for three months when Freda was born, but Melissa hadn't returned to her home, and her father, until Freda had been walking and talking. By then, she'd had time to prepare her story, her lies, and it had been far easier to explain to her old friends that she was a widow with a child, than to reveal that she'd been intimate with a man before the banns were called in church.

Now her scandalous past was about to be exposed. All the lies her parents had concocted to save them from the shame of their daughter having a child out of wedlock were about to be unraveled, and though she'd pessimistically imagined this day a thousand times, the reality was going to be more catastrophic than even her worst nightmares. Still, she'd never been one to shirk her responsibilities and she needed to be as strong as Michael believed her to be, for the sake of her daughter.

She rang for a maid to bring her water and to help her change out of her crumpled gown. The servants would be spreading the gossip below stairs by now, and Frederick would have been taken upstairs to a bedroom. The maid would know which one, because Melissa desperately needed to speak with Frederick, alone. Needed to hear what had prevented him from returning that morning and speaking to her father. Needed to know that he hadn't simply run away at the thought of being wed to her for the rest of his life. Because, in her lowest moments, she'd envisioned him rushing to board a ship and leave England, and her, behind him.

Frederick had parted from her at the Worthington's ball at three in the morning. He'd vowed to be standing on the steps of her family's London townhouse in five hours' time to ask her father's permission to marry her. She'd been giddy with excitement when she'd said goodnight to her parents and retreated to her room, barely able to keep from blurting out that she was in love and about to be married. At first, Frederick had asked her to keep their whirlwind relationship a secret because someone had threatened his life, and he didn't want that unknown person to turn his focus onto Melissa.

But Frederick's investigator had caught the men following him and had, eventually, tracked down the sender of the threatening letters. Their information had been handed over to Scotland Yard the afternoon before the Worthington's ball, and Frederick had expected that the people involved, two acquaintances of Frederick's, would be arrested the next morning. Frederick would give his statement to the police about the criminal activities he'd unwittingly witnessed, the perpetrators would be jailed, and his life would no longer be in danger.

Giddy with relief, Frederick had whisked Melissa off to the greenhouse and asked her to marry him, as soon as possible. They'd hugged and kissed and had been carried away by passion when they had finally been able to declare their love for each other, and knowing that within a few weeks they would be husband and wife.

Neither had wanted to wait another moment to be together so their coupling had been fast and fumbling, with Frederick apologizing over and over in the aftermath and promising that the next time they made love they would be in a comfortable bed, not on a conservatory bench, and he would shower her with love and bring her unimaginable pleasure. That second coupling never came to pass, as Frederick didn't arrive home that night. It took his staff, and family, a day or so to understand that he wasn't staying with a friend and had actually vanished on a London street in the early hours of what should have been Melissa's betrothal day.

Now, all she could think of was getting to Frederick and demanding answers to the questions that had run through her head night after night, month after month. Had she been too innocent, too clueless during their brief coupling that he'd been repulsed or appalled and decided to run way rather than marry her? She tormented herself with those questions for years and yet, now that she might finally learn the truth, she was terrified of the answers.

She clung to the idea that Michael didn't seem repulsed whenever he kissed her and always had great difficulty dragging himself away from her mouth, and her body. It wasn't as if she'd gained any more experience in being bedded by a man since her one and only night with Frederick. Huh, hardly a night. More like an hour, which was all the time she'd been able to sneak away from her mother's watchful eye. But from the first time she and Michael had kissed, she'd known that it was different. Deeper, more meaningful, and far more addictive. She'd wanted to wrap her arms around Michael's muscled body and never let go, and if Michael's ragged breathing and tight grapes on her waist had been anything to go by, he'd been similarly affected.

But all her dreams of spending her nights in Michael's bed, as his wife, were about to be shattered and she had none to blame but herself. She'd imagined that she and Frederick would have many long years together and had willingly given herself to him, her infatuation, her first love. Ironically, her mother had trouble conceiving at all during her many years of marriage, which was why she only had one sibling, a sister who was nine years younger than Melissa. Yet she'd conceived Freda during one youthful joining. She'd never regret having Freda, the biggest joy in her life, but she did regret the years she'd been forced to spend as a virtual recluse when she'd been carrying her babe and until Freda could be presented as the child of a widow. Her sin couldn't be allowed to tarnish the life of her younger sister, or diminish her chances of making a good match when she made her coming out.

Yes, she'd understood all the reasons she and Freda had spent her babyhood with little contact with her family, but that hadn't stopped her empty heart from aching or her mind from imagining Freda with a loving father, and she with an adoring husband.

When the maid knocked and opened the door, Melissa called her inside and gave her instructions about having warm water brought up for her to wash in, and for a fresh gown to be brought out of the cupboard. She desperately needed to get to Frederick, and even if he was ill her feminine pride wouldn't let her approach her former love until she somewhat resembled the bubbly young girl she'd been before he left.

"Mary," she said casually, "what was the news from the latest arrivals?"

"Oooh, you mean the man in the wheeled chair? Well, Mason told the housekeeper that the poor man was grabbed on the street and taken away many years ago." Mary laid a lemon day gown on the bed and sighed. "Whoever took 'im must've been a cruel person, my lady, because the man looks ready to have the preacher say words over 'im."

Melissa gasped. "Is he that sick?"

"I ain't seen 'im, meself, but the under-footmen who carried him upstairs to his room said 'e looked like he wouldn't live to see another sunrise. Poor gent. And he came all this way to find someone, 'e said."

Melissa held her hand to her face so Mary wouldn't hear her shocked gasps. "Did...did the gentleman say who he had come to see?"

"Nah, too sick to say too much. But the other gent, the navy one, he told His Grace where the man had been found and 'ow he'd been put on a ship and sent to England."

"Which...which bedchamber was the gentleman taken to?"

"Her Grace asked one of her family to shift rooms so they could put the sick gent close to the stairs. Easier to fetch for 'im and for his carrying 'is chair if the gent is well enough to leave." The maid shuddered. "Not likely he'll leave though.'

Melissa waited until the maid had finished in her room before she stepped into the corridor, forcing herself to appear calm. Her stomach was tied in knots and her feet wanted to run, not walk, to Frederick's room. A dozen questions were buzzing around her mind and she was desperate to get answers before she had to speak with Michael. Her breath hitched and she wrapped her arms around her abdomen. She was going to lose Michael. Lose any chance of being his wife. Lose the chance of Freda having a wonderful man as her father.

A sob bubbled up and escaped. She covered her mouth with both hands and looked around. Luckily the corridor remained empty. She stiffened her spine and hurried across the stairwell opening and stopped before the first room in the east wing. She lifted her hand to knock but stopped, and listened. Silence. Yet someone, most likely a footman, would have been left sitting with Frederick, even if everyone else was downstairs discussing arrangements for Frederick's care, or hopefully fetch a doctor as soon as the snow stopped.

She plucked up her courage and turned the knob. No voice told her to stop so she pushed opened the door. A footman sprang to his feet when she walked to the bed. "You may go, thank you. I will sit with his lordship."

The man wavered between listening to her, a visitor, or following the orders issued by the duke. She smiled reassuringly and the footman gave her a respectful nod and left the room, closing the door behind him. She heaved a sigh of relief and lowered herself into the chair vacated by the footman.

Frederick's eyes were closed and his chest rose and fell in shuddery movements with each labored breath. She slid her hand across the bed linen and laid it gently on top of Frederick's. Touching him felt strange, and yet familiar. Four years ago, she'd reveled in the feel of his muscled arm under her hand when he'd led her to the dance floor, or when they'd walked together in the park. Loved touching his fingers on the rare occasions they'd been gloveless and alone. And she could still recall the way her heart had raced when, on their last night together, Frederick had arranged for them to be alone for more than a few minutes and she'd run her hands over his bared arms and chest. Even then they'd not been able to risk removing all their clothing.

The only man she'd seen naked was Michael and that had been less than a month ago. They'd been on several outings together, danced at balls, and done all the things society expected from a courting couple, though for four months she'd refuted that idea, and the label, because she'd thought she and Michael were friends, nothing more. He was an extraordinarily handsome man and Melissa had imagined he'd have his pick of a long list of ladies whenever he decided to marry. She was a widow, supposedly, and had a little girl to worry about. Not the young and innocent bride highly ranked gentleman sought for marriage. Yet to her wonderment, Michael, kind and loving Michael, had selected her. Had asked her to marry him, and when she'd expressed all the arguments against him marrying her and for marrying a debutante, Michael had laughed.

"Why would I want that," he'd said. "Eating breakfast across from a simpering chit who could only discuss ribbons and bonnets when I could sit with you and discuss politics and geography and books. And why would I want to take a terrified girl to my bed and spend the next year trying to reassure her that everything we did between the sheets was completely natural and enjoyable when I could have you with me. Skin to skin, face to face, and with love in our eyes."

She'd cried at his beautiful words and agreed to be his wife, and she'd smiled all day and every day since that night. Until today, until Frederick had been carried inside the duke's house and all her dreams and hopes became as temporary as the snow outside this house's front door. By tomorrow, the snow, and her happiness, will have melted and be trampled under the feet of departing guests. Stories would be carried with them about the stranded travelers and people would speculate on the relationship between Melissa, Frederick, Michael, and of course Freda, who all shared the surname of Brandon.

Frederick's fingers tightened around hers and Melissa gasped. "You're awake."

"Is that you, Melissa?" His voice was hoarse and she leaned closer to catch his words.

"Yes." She covered their linked hands with her other one and tightened her grip. "I thought you were dead. We all did."

"I imagined that scenario and I worried about you. So much. I tried so hard to escape those pirates." He stopped to draw breath, looking drained.

"Don't try to speak until you're stronger, Frederick. You need to rest."

His fingers tightened slightly on hers again, though he had little strength in his grip. "There is no time, Melissa. I'm dying."

"No, no." She shook her head. "You're going to get better and then we'll talk about what happened."

He shifted a little on the bed and groaned. "Huh. What happened was that I was far from a gentleman. I took your virginity and didn't come back for four years. No chance to address your father and ask for your hand." He coughed, his thin frame shaking with the effort. "Came home to try to fix that. To marry you. If I lived long enough." His eyes closed briefly before he said, "Unless you have already married."

"No, I'm not married." She swiped at the tears flowing down her cheeks.

"And were..." He coughed again, unable to stop, and blood spittle flecked the sheet tucked up to his chin. Melissa gasped.

"Oh, Frederick." She stood and took the cloth on the bedside table, dipped into the basin of water, and gently wiped his chin.

He gave a small smile. "Thank you." He stared at her intently. "But I must know. Were there any consequences after our night together?" His shoulders sagged into the linens, as if even that much conversation had sapped his strength. "Not a day went by that I didn't think of you, and worried about you." He coughed again "Worried that there could be a child and that you were left to explain by yourself. To cope without the support of a husband. Without me."

She gave him a sad smile. How typical of Frederick to have worried all this time about her, despite how much he had obviously suffered. He'd been sweet and considerate towards her, despite many in society thinking him distant, perhaps even a little cold. During their brief time of physical intimacy, Frederick had taken great pains to explain each step before he progressed and he'd succeeded in his aim to be a patient and gentle teacher. She'd been totally enamored of him, and had loved him even more for the care he'd taken with her body and her emotions.

Holding her handkerchief to her mouth, she tried to smother her distress, and her sobs, when she saw this previously strong man lying as helpless as a child in his sick bed. Guilt tore at her that she'd ever been so shallow as to listen to the vicious gossip that had abounded after Frederick disappeared. Some speculated that he'd run away to avoid a woman, a marriage, or debts, or any other thing the Ton considered would give him reason to flee England without a word. Because she and Frederick had not been attended many events together, the gossips never considered that she might be offended at their wild conjectures about Frederick's behavior, and his faults and foibles. But through it all she'd clung to the belief that something dreadful had happened to stop Frederick returning that morning. Only in her darkest moments in bed, alone and pregnant, had her mind wandered to thoughts of him leaving due to her inadequacies in bed, or because he'd suddenly realized she wasn't wife material. After Freda was born, her wonderings had been replaced by anger and she'd been furious with Frederick for leaving to raise their child alone. And of leaving her to invent stories and tell lies to explain why she had no man supporting her.

For a few moments, she considered her options. If she denied that Freda was his child, would he be relieved, or would he be sad that he was leaving this world with no offspring to carry his name. She'd lied so many times to protect her beautiful daughter that one more would be nothing, yet she couldn't force herself to deny Freda, their beautiful child, to her father.

She nodded. "Yes. We have a daughter, a beautiful daughter called Freda. Named after you, Frederick."

A loud gasp from behind her startled Melissa and she jumped to her feet. She spun towards the door and discovered Michael standing between her and the door, less than five paces behind her chair. She'd been so caught up in Frederick's question she hadn't heard him enter the room. She stretched out a hand towards Michael but he stopped frozen on the spot, while his gaze swiveled between she and Frederick, back and forth.

"Frederick?" His question carried a wealth of pain and torment. "Frederick is Freda's father? Oh, my God. Why didn't I see it sooner? How could I have been so blind? Especially as you kept his name." Frederick called feebly to his brother, but Michael shook his head and didn't move towards the bed. Melissa stepped towards him and he held up his hand, palm out, while he heaved in several strained breaths. He walked towards Frederick, taking a wide berth around Melissa to the far side of the bed, and not meeting her gaze.

When Michael reached Frederick's side, he took his brother's thin hand in his and bowed his head. "It seems, brother, that we've both learned some startling news."

Frederick beckoned Melissa closer and she stood opposite Michael, staring at him across Frederick's bed and willing him to meet her eyes, to look at her with the admiration and adoration she'd become accustomed to recently.

"Freda?" Frederick looked between them both, begging more information.

Melissa slumped back onto the chair. "Yes, Frederick. Not only do you have a daughter, named her Freda after her father, but I've been calling myself a widow with the surname of Brandon." She waved a hand in the air, unable to find the words to explain her panic and fear when she'd discovered that was *enceinte* and that the father was missing, presumed dead. "I didn't know what else to do." She sighed. "Besides, I wanted your child to carry your name, both your names, because I was certain you would return." She swallowed. "I never believed you were dead, Frederick. Never."

Michael nodded. "For what it's worth, Frederick, I too always believed we'd find you." He shook his head. "We tried so hard, for years, but you'd vanished without a trace." He placed his hand on Frederick's shoulder. "I'm so glad that you're here."

Frederick shook his head, and then moaned. "But not for long, unfortunately." His thin frame shook when another coughing fit hit him, his breath wheezing in and out with a grating sound like an unsharpened saw. The agony of it terrified Melissa.

"No, no, don't say such things, Frederick. We'll get a doctor here as soon as the snow clears. The doctor will make you better. I know he will." She sponged Fredrick's sweating brow with a damp cloth and was relieved when his shoulders relaxed back onto the linen sheet and his breathing evened out. "And then, when you're feeling better, you can meet your daughter."

Frederick grimaced. He looked at Michael. "No doctor can help me now, Michael. I'm dying. Doctors on the continent said I'd been kept too long on the ship. Too long in chains in the damp hold. Too little food." He wheezed again and Melissa held her breath, hoping it wouldn't trigger another coughing attack. "Consumption," Frederick muttered. He reached for her hand, grasping her fingers in his own trembling ones. "I'm so sorry. Please forgive me, Melissa."

"No," she cried, swiping at the tears racing down her cheeks. "Nothing is your fault." She shook her head. "Nothing, do you hear me. You'll feel better tomorrow. I'll bring Freda to meet her father." Michael reached across the bed and pressed a dry handkerchief into her hand. She blew her nose noisily, past caring about behaving in a lady-like manner.

"Brother," Frederick said, appealing to Michael. "Please listen to me. Those pirates may have robbed me a long life, but I will die in peace now, knowing that I will be leaving a legacy." He gave a wan smile. "A child. A daughter." His eyes closed and his breathing slowed.

Melissa's breath caught. She was terrified that his chest would stop moving and she'd be powerless to revive him. "Frederick,' she screamed, laying her hands on his chest.

Michael was also calling his bother's name, over and over, and though his tone was more a command from one gentleman to another, rather than a panicked scream as hers had been, she saw the torment on Michael's face.

Frederick's frame shook again as he drew in several rattling breaths. Melissa's knees went weak and she sank back onto the chair and openly sobbed, while Michael bent over the bed and pressed a kiss to his brother's cheek. When he stood upright, Melissa saw tears running down his cheek too, but they went unheeded because Michael's gaze was fixed on his brother's gaunt face, as if he was willing Frederick to open his eyes, to live.

After several excruciating seconds, Frederick's eyes fluttered open and he spoke softly. "You must both help me."

"Anything," Melissa said, while at the same time Michael said, "Whatever you need."

"I've had four years to think about this, to make plans for when I returned." He paused for breath. "I know who kidnapped me, and why."

Michael made a strangled noise. "Who? Who did it? When I find them, I'll make them pay for taking you away from your family." He glanced across at her and frowned. "For taking you away from the lady you loved." He rubbed this forehead. "For robbing you of the years you deserved married to a lady who loved you in return. And for robbing Freda of her father."

Melissa opened her mouth to speak, but could form no words. Yes, she had loved Frederick four years ago and had mourned his disappearance, but since meeting Michael she'd realized that what she'd shared with Frederick had been the sort of exciting and joyous love shared by two young people who hadn't known each other well, but had naively believed that they'd have many years together. A lifetime to learn more about each other and to grow into maturity together.

She bowed her head, overcome with guilt and grief. Guilt that she'd shared more of herself, physically and emotionally, with

Michael over the last six months than she'd ever shared with Frederick, despite having known the elder brother for a longer time in terms of months or years, due to Frederick being the heir to the estate and Michael having been the second brother who'd left to make his own way in the world.

Michael laid his hand gently on his brother's arm. "I promise that they will be caught, and punished. Every damn one of the bastards."

Frederick nodded. "Good. But for your benefit, not mine. Because theses men have no conscience. They will not stop, even after I'm dead. You are now in danger." He sucked in a breath. "And my daughter will be too, if they come to know of her existence."

Melissa couldn't smother her gasp in time, and both men turned to her with sympathy in their eyes. Frederick shifted one the bed, looking unsettled and distressed, and Michael's mouth hung open in shock.

"Why," she begged. "Why would Freda be in danger? And Michael?"

"Those men, those pirates, were in the employ of a powerful group here in England. Peers, greedy and desperate men." Another coughing fit interrupted his speech.

Melissa again sponged Frederick's face, shocked by the heat radiating through the damp cloth. His fever must be incredibly high. She wrung out the cloth and placed it beside the basin of water, watching Frederick gasp for breath and his face contort with pain. She shared a look of painful realization with Michael.

What Frederick said was most likely true. He was dying. Even if the snow stopped and they could send someone for the doctor, starvation and consumption had already taken its toll on Frederick's body.

"You must rest, brother. We can talk more in the morning."

Frederick grabbed at his brother's arm. "A short rest, no more. I must record everything, before it's too late." His sentences were again punctuated by brief stops, while he caught his breath. "Witnesses. Magistrate. Write it down, before I die."

Michael frowned for a moment. "Sherwyn," he then said, looking at Melissa with a question in his eyes.

"Yes, yes. The duke is the biggest local landowner, so most likely the magistrate."

"We're all taking refuge in the house of the Duke of Sherwyn," Michael said. "He's a good man. And his cousin, Richard, is an earl and is also staying here for their family celebrations. They can stand witness to whatever you have to report."

Frederick gave a weak nod. "Wake me in two hours. Please. And Melissa, would you come too." His eyes closed. Melissa nodded at Michael and they both turned towards the door. A maid, thankfully not a young one, was waiting to enter and Melissa stopped to speak with her, reminding her to sponge his brow and to keep him as cool and comfortable as possible. When the maid assured her that she had experience nursing people with breathing problems, Melissa sighed with relief. Her feelings were echoed by Michael, whose shoulders relaxed for the first time since he'd entered his brother's room. He thanked the maid politely and profusely for taking good care of his brother over the next two hours.

"If anything happens, if the gentleman worsens, please ring for me immediately," Michael said. "I'll be speaking with His Grace downstairs."

Melissa understood Michael's reluctance to leave his brother, considering how fragile Frederick had looked, sunk deep into the mattress and with his face paler than the sheets that enclosed him. She wanted to take his hand, to comfort him, yet her disclosure about Freda's parentage hung like a dark cloud between them and she had no idea how, or when, she could explain it to him without seeing his expression turn to disgust for her of giving herself to Frederick before being married.

She considered her relationship with Michael as different, because she'd presented herself as a widow. A lady far removed from the naive and excitable young lady she'd been four years ago. But would Michael see it that way? Or was the closeness that had built up over the last months about to be shattered. Destroyed by the knowledge that she had lain with own brother and had never revealed that to him, not even when they'd been in bed, skin-to-skin, and as close as two human beings could be.

3

*M*ichael took Melissa's arm when they left Frederick's room. He was still trying to come to grips with the news that his present lover had been intimate with his brother, and that they had a child together. He guided her to another wing, surreptitiously watching to make sure they were alone, and led her to his bedchamber. The room was small, a bachelor's room that was obviously only called into service when Sherwyn had houseguests, or stranded travelers. He helped her settle into the armchair while he perched on the end of his bed, his legs spread wide either side of her skirts.

He reached for her hand. "Melissa, I only have one question."

She squeezed his fingers. "I'm sure you have a lot more than one question." She sighed. "I'm sorry, Michael. I started to tell you a dozen times."

He lightly shook her fingers. "I can't lie. It was a shock learning the identity of Freda's father that way." He sighed. "I do wish you'd had the courage to tell me before this, but only because I've been waiting for you to trust me enough to tell me about Freda's mystery father." He bent forward and brushed his lips across hers. "Nothing you tell me will ever make me love you less. You're a wonderfully warm and loving woman and I know you could never have done anything terrible."

Melissa's breath hitched on a sob. "But I have done something terrible, and I don't know if you'll be able to forgive me."

"Try me, sweetheart."

"I lied about being a widow. Lied to protect Freda. I didn't want her to be scorned because of her mother's mistakes."

He frowned. "Are you saying that... whatever you shared was some sort of mistake?" He sucked in a breath. "Please tell me Frederick didn't force you?"

She shook her head. "No, no, of course not. Frederick was kind and sweet." She sighed. "You must understand, I was young and infatuated and Frederick and I were going to announce our betrothal." She blotted her face with a handkerchief. "We ... Frederick and I ... only..." She cleared her throat. "It was only one time. We snuck away from everyone at a ball to discuss how Frederick would approach my father later that morning to tell him that we wished to marry. You didn't know my father, but he could be a difficult man. Liked to make all the decisions for our family and expected to be obeyed, immediately and with no discussions." She gave a small smile. "Your brother was much braver than me, and more optimistic about my father's acceptance of our news. I expected that my father would say no, simply because he hadn't been the one to decide that Frederick and I would marry."

"My darling, it matters little to me how many times you and Frederick ... were intimate." He snorted. "Well, perhaps if I am being completely truthful, I'm a little relieved that your relationship with my brother, physically at least, wasn't ongoing. It makes it somewhat easier to ask my question."

She raised her eyebrows. "Isn't that enough scandalous revelations for one day?"

He shook his head. "I need to know if you still love Frederick, especially after seeing him again. Knowing that he lives."

More tears trickled down her cheeks. "I fear that he won't be with us for much longer, Michael." She wiped her eyes with the damp linen square she'd been scrunching in her free hand. "But to answer your question, no, I no longer love your brother in that way, and even if he recovers from his illness, I couldn't be with him again. Not physically. Not when I love another." She stared at him, her eyes full of sincerity. "Not when I'm in desperately in love with you."

He stood and pulled her into his arms. "Oh, thank God," he murmured into her lemon-smelling hair. He leaned back so he could see her eyes when he added, "Because I couldn't give you up, even for a member of my family." He put his lips an inch from hers and whispered, "Though if you'd said you still loved Frederick, I would have found the strength, somehow, to wish you both well." He pulled back and stared at her. "Because I love you both, and want the best for both of you."

She kissed him, softy and sweetly, and his heart swelled in his chest and he could barely breathe. Losing Frederick, not being able to locate him, had destroyed a part of his soul and left a gaping hole in his heart. Meeting Melissa, falling in love with her and having his love returned had helped him to heal. Helped him look forward to the future, instead of dreading the future and the day Frederick would be discovered, dead.

"Michael, I would never have given myself to Frederick if I hadn't love him."

"I know that."

"But what we shared four years ago was an immature sort of love. Frederick and I barely knew each other because of my father's rigid rules about women's behavior. Our social life was restricted to events that my father considered proper. Not too flamboyant, and certainly not too much fun." She smiled. "It was a wonder that Frederick and I even met. Musical evenings were my father's first choice for our outings, and as you know, most bachelors abhor them and avoid them at all cost." She sucked in a breath. "Frederick had been dragged there, objecting strongly, by a friend who needed male support in his wooing of a sheltered young lady. We bumped into each other, literally, while trying to find a place to hide from the next round of screeching singing and horrifyingly bad harp playing."

Michael smiled at the image. "Frederick loves music, but loathes listening to it be butchered by terrified debutantes who have no ear for the pieces and are bullied into performing by pushing mamas. We made a pact when we were young men, newly out in society, that we'd invent excuses to avoid any, and all, musical commitments that our mother made on our behalf."

"Yes," Melissa said with a smile. "He told me. After that, if we were at the same party, we'd try to escape together to a quieter place, even for only a few minutes." She rested her forehead on his shoulder. "Those few minutes of freedom meant the world to me. Minutes away from the watchful eyes of my parents when I could escape their criticisms and speak to a person and be treated as an equal. That so rarely happened in my own home." She lifted her head and he saw sadness and regret in her eyes. "I think Frederick proposed to me as a way of freeing us both from the constraints put upon us by our families. And of course I accepted, grateful that I would be exchanging my restrictive home for a life with your brother, kind and considerate Frederick."

All he could do was nod, wishing he'd known her then so he could have been the one to remove her from her father's restraints, and yet grateful to his brother for proposing to her and opening up another way of life for Melissa, because she was a vibrant and passionate woman whose nature would have suffocated in a strict home environment.

She touched his cheek and he turned his face into her palm. "Michael, I swear to you that, though my love for Frederick might not have been the passionate love I feel for you, I did admit him greatly and I would have made him a good wife. My main regret when Freda was born was that Frederick wasn't there to see the miracle that they'd created together. And the Freda would most likely spend her life never knowing her father, or what happened to him."

He touched his tongue to her palm and she shivered. "I know, my love. I know you would have been a good wife; the same way you've been a wonderful mother." He kissed her, long and lovingly, until her body softened and she relaxed into him and their kiss. "And I know you'll be a wonderful wife when we marry."

She broke away and looked up at him in surprise. "You cannot still want to marry me, not after learning of my lies and deceit. Many will label me a fallen woman for lying with a man before marriage."

"Nobody will call you such names, my love, because no one needs to know that you're not a widow. We'll work it out. Trust me."

"Oh, Michael, I do trust you. And I do love you. More than I can ever say. But if we marry, you'll be tainted by my past."

"Wait, Melissa. Wait until we have all the facts from Frederick, and he's spoken with the duke. Let's not rush into any decisions about our future yet." He kissed her softly, but he could already feel her pulling away from him. Not that he would let her go far, not now that he'd found the woman he'd waited for his entire life.

"Come, sweetheart. You see your daughter while I ask Sherwyn to visit Frederick." He walked her to the sitting room, where her daughter launched herself at her mother's legs and pulled her inside to show her the game Freda and the children were playing. Freda waved her tiny fingers at him and giggled. He smiled. From the first moment he'd met the little imp, they'd bonded. He adored her mischievous grins, her never-ending questions, and her sweet hugs.

Knowing that Freda was his niece made her all the more precious, and made him even more determined to keep any hint of scandal away from both Freda and Melissa. An enquiry to the nearest footman pointed him in the direction of his host's office. He knocked on the duke's door and Sherwyn bade him enter and waved him to a seat before his enormous desk.

"Thank you for seeing me, Your Grace. Frederick, Lord Brandon, requests that you visit his chamber, if you wouldn't mind. He is anxious to share the story of his kidnapping with someone in authority, and I assume that you are the local magistrate when in residence."

The duke nodded. "I'll assist in any way I can. And Richard, my cousin, can stand witness to your brother's revelations. We will do everything we can to help you track down the men who kidnapped your brother."

"Thank you, Your Grace. And may I say how much we appreciate your hospitality." He sighed. "I pray that Frederick will recover enough to travel on with us when the bridge is repaired. Returning home with my brother would lift the spirits of my family, especially my mother. The stress of the past four years while we searched for Frederick has taken a toll on her health."

"Brandon, you must prepare yourself for a worsening of your brother's condition. He told me when he arrived that he was dying. Though the road may be passable in a day or two if the snow stops, it will take a week to repair the bridge." Sherwyn's shoulders sagged. "The chances of your brother returning to your home and greeting his parents are slim."

Tears pricked Michael's eyelids, but he forced them away. "I've feared that my brother was dead on and off for four years, Your Grace. Now that I've seen him, spoken with him, and held his hand, I plan on enjoying each precious moment that I have left with him. I cannot think about his passing. There will be time to mourn, truly mourn him, later."

"I understand." The duke rose. "I will find my cousin and meet you in your brother's room in an hour."

Michael dipped his head. "Thank you, Your Grace."

"Please, call me Sherwyn. After all, we are related somewhere along the line, aren't we?"

"Distant cousins, I think."

"Family is important to me, Brandon. Very important. I've learned to value each and every member of my family, immediate and extended." He put his hand on Michael's shoulder as they walked towards the door. "Whatever you need, just ask."

"You may regret saying that." Michael smiled faintly. "I have a feeling that I will be needing all the help I can get if I'm to get justice for the wrongs suffered by my brother."

They parted in the corridor, Sherwyn to enlist his cousin help as a witness to Frederick's testimony and Michael to find Melissa. She should be present when Frederick's testimony was given, because she had suffered the most after the kidnapping. An unmarried woman carrying a child, most likely forced to hide from society by leaving the security of her parents' home.

He found Melissa in the sitting room, surrounded by children while she read them a story. Freda sat on the settee close to her mother, leaning forward to look at the pictures in the book her mother held. All the children were enthralled with the story, and the story teller, and Michael's heart swelled with pride that the woman he loved, the woman he intended taking as his wife, was so incredibly warm and generous and a wonderful mother. If...when...they had their own children, they would be loved by both parents in the same way his own parents had lavished love on their offspring.

When Melissa had finished and the children run off to their next game, he explained about their upcoming meeting when the duke and the earl would witness Frederick's statement. It took a few minutes, but she agreed to come with him. Perhaps hearing the entire story would help Melissa heal.

4

Michael looked at the people witnesses gathered around Frederick's bed and was overcome with grief that this telling of his brother's story had to happen at all. He longed to charge downstairs and ride away from the duke's snow bound estate and begin his hunt for the unknown foe who had kidnapped his brother and ruined many lives in the process. When he caught up with their enemy, his first instinct would be to put his hands around the man's neck, or men's necks, if more than one peer was involved, and squeeze the life out of them, in the same way that a four-year long search for Frederick had drained the joy out of their family.

Melissa squeezed his hand and, on his other side, the duke clapped him on the back. Their unspoken show of support had his eyes filling with tears and he blinked hard to push them away. Time enough for grieving later, because for now, his brother lived and he needed Michael's help.

Frederick cleared his throat. "Thank you all for helping me clear this matter up before..." He broke off in a coughing fit.

Michael said, "Please do not voice it, Frederick. I cannot bear it."

Frederick's thin and wrinkled hand reached for Michael's and he took it and gave a gentle squeeze to show that he stood squarely behind Frederick, no matter what he asked.

Frederick gave them a weak smile. "I want you all to know how grateful I am to have returned home in time to give testimony against the criminals who held me prisoner." His words were interspersed with wheezing breaths. "Your Grace," he said, looking at Sherwyn. "If you write down my story, I will sign it so that as soon as the weather clears, you can send it to the authorities. I need these criminals caught before they turn their attention to other members of my family." He turned his head and looked at Michael. "You are in danger."

"Certainly," the Duke of Sherwyn replied as he nodded towards his cousin who seated himself with a traveling desk beside the bed. "The earl will record your testimony and we will all sign it. You have my word that as soon as possible, the letter will be dispatched to London to a man I trust implicitly in the Home Office."

Frederick nodded and began his story while Michael, and the other witnesses all leaned forward to catch each whispery word. "When barely past my majority, I used a small inheritance to buy a run-down sugar plantation in the West Indies. I sent a man I trusted to be manager and he did well for me." He glanced at Michael again. "For us."

Michael frowned. "I don't understand."

"Our parents were very young when they had us, Michael, and could be expected to live a long time. You were still away at school when I inherited that money unexpectedly. Father and I agreed that it could be something that would give us an income when we were old enough to marry, and father added some money to the pot."

Michael shook his head. "I didn't know anything of this."

"To be truthful, the plantation was pushed to the back of my mind when I became old enough to enjoy London and all the delights available to a young man." Sherwyn snorted his agreement and Michael smiled. "Several years passed before the plantation was restored enough to begin making any income so, though I was pleased, that news from my manager still wasn't of any immediate concern for me, or you. So I waited, hopeful that the next year's news would be good for us. But I received no further correspondence from my manager. I became alarmed for his safety and wrote letters to the governor out there and several other contacts who might have heard some news. Eventually, I learned that my manager was dead, most likely murdered. An investigation revealed no clue to his assassin, and no one could explain why correspondence to and from the plantation abruptly stopped. My letters to the manager were never found, and any reports of letters might have been drafting to send to me during his last weeks had also vanished."

Frederick closed his eyes and waited until he'd caught his breath. "I did learn, however, that my small plantation was about to earn us a sudden and escalated income. Turned out that my small harbor was the best place for a new port out of any others on the islands. Surveyors hired by the government had discovered this, but decided they could make a tidy sum of money by pretending that the plantation was owned by one of their own family. With my manager out of the picture, they persuaded the newly arrived governor that the money could be paid to them on behalf their relatives and could be invested back into the plantation, thus ensuring faster development around the new port that the governor had been sent to build."

Sherwyn interrupted. "Surely they knew their plan would unravel when you made enquiries about your manager and your property?"

Frederick nodded. "They planned on being far away, with Britain's investment money, long before I could push for more of an investigation. Distance was on their side." He sucked in three deep breaths, while the witnesses stood silent, spellbound by his tale. "Unfortunately for those thieves, I had asked two friends who were going to work in the islands to make themselves known to my manager and send me an unbiased report on the situation." Once again, he glanced at Michael. "I thought I was being a good overseer for our investment, yet all I did was sign my own death warrant.

"The men had contacts with ship owners of all sorts and they sent men a band of pirates to capture me on the street in London and remove me. The original idea was to keep me long enough for the search to continue, dropping hints here and there in ports to say I'd been seen." He shuddered. "What actually happened was that eight men died on the pirate's ship of a fever and they kept me, chained, to do the navvy work for them. I scrubbed decks and mended sails and prayed that I would find a way to escape. My release came after the pirate ship lost a mast and had to anchor in a sheltered cove, which happened to be on an island used by our Royal Navy for their own repairs." He waved a feeble hand in the air. "They arranged for me to be sent here, though I knew the chances of me surviving the voyage to England were slim. I'd been starved too long, and my lungs inhaled too much damp air for me to fully recover. But, Michael, I knew the original crooks would come after you the moment I was reported as deceased. With you gone, they hoped to escape any charges of criminal activity. And, the two surveyors are both younger sons of respected British families, both now living back in England and spending money freely. Money that should be mine, and yours."

"Good heavens," Sherwyn said. "I can see how they would think themselves safe. With any one who can testify against them gone, the courts would have a hard time convicting them, especially if they have the influence of their family's behind them." He gripped Michael's shoulder. "It's a blessing in disguise that you were strand by the snow storm. At least here you are safe."

"And Melissa," Frederick said, peering up at her.

"Me," Melissa said in surprise. "What would they have to fear from me?"

"My will was made years ago, yet it states that any property belonging to me will be divided between any family I have. A wife, or children."

Melissa leaned over the bed and frantically whispered, "But I'm not your wife."

Frederick peered at Sherwyn. "With the duke's aid, I hope to rectify that while I have time. Your Grace, I trust our secrets will remain between us."

Sherwyn nodded. "No word will leave this house, other than the words that you have dictated for us to send to the Home Office. My family and I have been in ... difficult... circumstances more than once ourselves and therefore understand the necessity for discretion. There will be no gossip, no scandalous tales taken away and spread about. You have my word."

"Melissa was about to become my wife when I was taken. To my shame, I left her as an unmarried woman with a baby. I beg you to take pity on me, on us all, and send for someone who can marry us as soon as the roads clear."

Melissa gasped and Michael shook his head.

"Even if there is time," Melissa said, "how will that help?"

Frederick reached for Melissa's hand and held it. "Please, my dear. Let me rectify my greatest sin. For four years I have worried about you and berated myself for leaving you alone, possibly with child. By marrying now, you will inherit my half of the plantation. Our daughter will inherit. The port is apparently built and thriving, so even if the original money is never recovered, you shall be a rich woman. And my daughter..." He broke off to swipe a trembling hand across this face and remove the tears flowing down his cheeks. "You cannot imagine how much joy you have brought me with the news that I will at least be leaving a daughter when I finally succumb to this wretched lung infection."

Michael stood silent, no knowing what to say. Yes, he wanted his brother to die in peace after all he'd suffered, but by marrying Melissa, Frederick would put her out of his won reach. She would be in mourning for a year or two and be unable to marry him, or even continue with the social life they'd been enjoying for the past months. The Ton would expect him to retreat and mourn with his parents at their home. The idea of going months without being able to see Melissa, or Freda, hurt more than any physical wound.

He shook his head. "No, no, Frederick. Please, not that." He slid his arm around Melissa's waist and was gratified that she leaned into him, as she always did. Then she recalled herself.

Melissa straightened, and stepped away from Michael, hands covering her mouth. She gave an agonized groan. "I don't know what to do."

Sobs shook Melissa's entire frame and Michael felt like the lowest of men. He reached for her but she backed away, tears running down her face, and sobbing uncontrollably.

Richard put down his writing desk and stood. "Mrs. Brandon, perhaps we can continue this discussion later, after you've rested. Would you like me to call Laura and Becca to help you?"

Melissa stared at the earl, wide-eyed, before she nodded. He moved to the bell-pull and rang for a maid, but a second later there was a knock on the door. The door opened and Laura and Becca stepped inside. Richard and Sherwin both shook their heads.

"I might have known," Richard said, taking his wife's arm and drawing her inside. "Listening at the keyhole again, my love?"

Despite the circumstances, Michael couldn't help but give a snort of laughter. Laura was known for her inquisitiveness and her sister, Becca, was known as a problem solver. The wonder was that they'd stayed silent outside the door for so long, and that their younger sister, Charlotte, hadn't also been party to their blatant spying. Though their prying was usually does with the best of intentions, as the Jamison siblings all had hearts of gold.

Michael had known the Jamison brothers at school and though he'd not had a lot of contact with them since he'd returned to London, he had spoken with them on a few occasions at balls and soirees recently. The two Jamison men and the St. Martin men often gathered as a protective circle around the women when they attended society events, after a madwoman had threatened the women's lives if Becca didn't hand over her incredibly accurate stock predictions.

Michael and Melissa had spoken with the group at several events lately, and Michael was thankful that, if they had to be snow-bound, they had become stranded at Sherwyn's estate. The duke was known as an honest, fair, and hard-working man, which relieved Michael in light of his brother's requests. He was confident that Melissa's unmarried status and Freda's parentage, would stay between these walls, though he wasn't confident that he'd be strong enough to see Melissa married to his brother, even if that marriage was detained to be a brief, and chaste, arrangement.

He looked over to where Melissa had been settled on a settee by

Becca and Laura and was thankful that her heart-wrenching sobs appeared to have abated somewhat. Frederick's eyes were closed and his breathing had evened out, so he was snatching a few much-needed moments of sleep.

Michael raked a hand through his hair. "God, what an unholy mess," he muttered.

Richard, standing close by, overheard him. As his cousin had done earlier, the earl gripped Michael's shoulder in a show of support.

"Take heart, Michael. It will all work out in the end. You can trust Sherwyn and I to take care of the official report, and to ensure that the perpetrators of your brother's imprisonment are brought to justice. No one will speak of any personal issues being sorted here outside this room. I want you to know that."

Michael nodded. "Thank you. I appreciate your help. If this had happened at my parent's house, if my brother had made it home, this entire situation would have quickly become fodder for the local gossips."

"And," Richard continued, "as you and Mrs. Brandon are so obviously in love, we will all try our damnedest to keep you two together."

Michael groaned. "Melissa. What am I going to do about her? I can't lose her, and yet I cannot deny my brother's request to finally marry Melissa and to recognize Freda as his child." He shook his head. When Sherwyn came to join them, Michael said, "I'm damned if I don't support my brother's request and crucified if I give the woman I love to him without a fight."

"I've been thinking," Sherwyn said. "Our family is related to an Archbishop who lives close to us. He can be trusted to keep quiet about what ever we ask him to do. When Frederick awakens, I will suggest to him that the Archbishop be brought here the moment the road opens. He can perform a simple marriage ceremony between Frederick and Melissa."

Michael scowled. "But that means a year of mourning."

The duke held up his hand." Hear me out. No one but those presently in this house will know when the marriage was performed.

Church recordings, and marriage certificates, are susceptible to moisture. If the archbishop's recorded dates become smudged, illegible, who will know besides us? That way, when your brother passes from us, the archbishop will lead us in a family service for him and afterwards..." The duke shrugged. "And if the archbishop then performs another wedding ceremony, once again with only those residing here as witnesses, the dates recorded may also be smudged by drops of water."

The earl smiled. "It happens all the time. Parchment becomes damp, dates fade in church record books. No one will ever know exactly what year Frederick and Melissa were married and..." He looked at Michael." No one will be surprised that you and Melissa secretly married recently, because anyone withers can see you two are meant to be together."

Michael's mind churned with the possibilities thrown up by the duke. "Can we pull it off without raising suspicion?"

"This is going to question the word of a duke and his duchess," Sherwyn said nonchalantly.

Michael wanted the duke's plan to work, wanted it desperately, yet the duke was a magistrate and an honest man. "You'd do this for me? For us?"

He duke and his cousin shared a knowing smile. "Wouldn't be the first time we've blurred the edges of legality for a worthy cause."

"Probably not the last either," Richard added with a grin. "We'll be delighted if there can be a happy ending after such a sad time. And I think Frederick will rest easier knowing that his brother is going to look after his beloved, and their daughter."

Michael's eyes filled and his heart swelled with anticipation and joy. To think that these men, and their wives, would stand by him, his brother, and the woman he wanted to marry made him emotional and grateful, though neither Cayle or Richard would appreciate a gentleman of their circles crying before them. He willed away his tears and tried to thank them again, but his throat was clogged and words wouldn't come.

Cayle cleared his throat. "Yes, well it will be our pleasure to arrange things here, but first you must get Mrs. Brandon to agree to the plan." The duke gestured to where his wife, Becca, patted Melissa's folded hands while Laura poured cups of tea from the tray a maid had delivered.

Michael looked at the three women, grateful that Becca and her sister were taking care of Melissa, whose face was as white as a sheet and her hands trembled so much that her cup shook and rattled on her saucer. How was he going to explain their plan to her when she was obviously in shock? Having your past love, and the father of your child, reappear when you'd given him up for dead would shock anyone, even a strong woman like Melissa.

Hell, his own hands were none too steady. Thank heavens the duke had been thinking clearly and had formulated a plan that might give his brother some peace in his last days, apart from possibly allowing he and Melissa to continue with their plans for the future. His own thoughts alternated between joy that his brother was alive, grief that he might only have a brief time to enjoy their reunion, and panic that Melissa might turn her back on him now. She'd revealed next to nothing about her previous relationship and he'd been unwilling to pressure her, assuming that she couldn't bear to relive the grief of losing the man she'd loved.

Though he'd had doubts about Melissa being married to her past love, he certainly didn't think less of her because no church held an official record of a marriage. Hypocritical of society to encourage a young man to sow his wild oats before marriage and yet blame and condemn a woman, the other half of their union, if a child was created. For that reason, many women who found themselves carrying a child out of wedlock crated a fictitious husband. Widows were accepted by society, unmarried mothers were shamed. He loathed the thought of Melissa and Freda being the subject of vicious gossip, so he applauded her for taking whatever path would have kept her, and her daughter, protected from ridicule.

Frederick's weak call from the bed startled them all. Melissa rushed back to his side and took his hand, holding it to her lips and placing a gentle kiss on the back of Frederick's wrinkled fingers.

Michael sucked in a ragged breath. He was an idiot, a blind fool. How could he not have considered that Melissa's love for Frederick had been so strong that the mere sight of him, here, and alive, had revived that love. She held Frederick's hand so tenderly and whispered so close to his ear, that Michael was immobilized by a of streak of raw and painful jealousy, immediately followed by a rush of overwhelming guilt. What sort of monster would envy his dying brother for having a warm and caring lady at his side, bending over him and caressing his cheek?

Oh, God, what would he do if Melissa's feelings for Frederick overshadowed the love she'd told him she held for him. And Sherwyn was about to put his idea to Frederick and gain his approval for fetching his distant cousin, the archbishop, to perform a marriage ceremony here, in this room, with Michael bearing witness. He doubted he'd be strong enough to watch the ceremony, even for his brother's sake, without knowing if Melissa was willing to carry through with the second part of Sherwyn's plan. If she'd carry the plan through to the end, to their own marriage.

He shook his head, willing away all negative thoughts. If Frederick said yes to the plan, he'd have a few days of peace and happiness, perhaps even a week. And after all he'd suffered, Frederick deserved to feel loved and wanted and if that meant ensuring that Frederick had the full attention of the woman and child Michael also loved, then he would stiffen his spine and paste a smile on his face. He stepped closer to the bed.

"While you've been resting," Sherwyn said, "I had an idea of how the inheritance you wish to leave for Melissa and Freda can be protected." He nodded towards Michael. "And how you can help your brother carry out your wishes."

Frederick's eyes glistened with tears. "Returning home and setting things to rights is all that kept me alive through those endless nights chained in the hold of the ship." He reached for the duke's hand. "I can die in peace if we can settle my financial affairs and ensure the safety of those I love."

All eyes went to Sherwyn as he explained, in a calm and efficient tone, how a marriage between Frederick and Melissa could take place. "The archbishop can perform the ceremony here, at your bedside, and all of us will be happy to stand witness. After that," he shrugged, "unpredictable things often happen to church registers. Leaky roofs cause water to ruin registry books, dates fade, and recordings become illegible. A marriage performed here, this week, might well appear to have taken place four years ago." The duke cleared his throat, twice. "After ...after..."

Frederick gave him a small smile. "You may say it aloud, Your Grace. After I die, which is likely to happen very soon." He sucked in deep, and obviously painful, breaths. The European medicos believed that I wouldn't survive the channel crossing. Every day I've drawn breath since landing in England has been an added blessing. It took all my willpower to make my lungs keep working until I could speak to someone from my family. Now, it's a matter of hours. Perhaps a day or two, until my lungs stop working."

Sherwyn gave a nod of understanding. "My estate manager has been out again to inspect the roads, and the bridge. Luckily, the archbishop lives in the other direction from the bridge, towards London. As soon as the road clears enough for horses, he will be escorted here by my men."

He slid his arm around Becca, his duchess, who had come to stand beside her husband. Michael was heartened to see that Cayle and Becca openly display their shared love, and to know that this marriage was based on a lot more than convention an convenience. These two supported each other wholeheartedly and was exactly the type of marriage he hoped for with Melissa. Sharing of the good times, and the bad, and standing together on important issues. He glanced at Richard and Laura. They also stood together, leaning into each other and with Laura's arm looped through the earl's elbow. Two marriages between peers that were so vastly different to the majority of the forced and unhappy society unions, and Michael was enthralled by their closeness and in awe of the care they obviously took to share everything and work as a team.

"But there is another part to my plan," Sherwyn continued. "After you die, Frederick," he stated gently, ignoring the soft noises of sorrow from the bystanders, "the archbishop can also perform another marriage ceremony. Your brother was on his way to your parents house to share the happy news that Melissa had consented to become his wife."

"Yes," Frederick nodded. "Michael was very honest about why they'd been en route to our visit our parents when it is still early December."

"Normally," Michael told Sherwyn and his family, his voice husky with emotion at the memories he shared with his brother of past Christmases at their family estate. Though they'd gathered of the past four years, conversation had centered on the latest reports in their search for Frederick, rather than Christmas. His news this year when he reached his parents would devastate them, because they'd held strong to the belief that Frederick still lived, especially his mother who had said time and again that she'd have sensed it if her eldest son had passed away. None of them had doubted her bond with her child, so they'd sent men and messages to every corner of the earth in their quest to bring him home.

"We'd...our family...Fredrick's and mine," Michael had to pause to regain his composure. "We came together only a few days before Christmas in years past, but they year I wanted my parents to get better acquainted with Melissa, and Freda, before the chaos of our extended family arriving."

"So, Your Grace, am I understanding you correctly? Your kin, the archbishop, would also be prepared to make the date of Michael's marriage to Melissa...unreadable?"

The duke nodded. "Yes, if they are wed quietly here, no one will know but us. That way, there will be no need for them to wait the customary year or two of mourning. Melissa and Freda, and their inheritance, will be far better protected if your widow and your daughter are under the protection of a husband, a man known to have strong principles and to friends with a group of likeminded gentlemen, one of whom happens to be the Duke of Sherwyn." He snorted. "Being a duke can be a burden, but the title also allows me a great deal of leeway when I want to do something." He shrugged. "So at times like these, why not use my title? Not that the archbishop will much coercing from me." He smiled. "He's more like one's favorite uncle than a man of the cloth, and he's quite a romantic."

Melissa's moan of distress had all eyes turning to her. "But...but... Your Grace, what you are suggesting is illegal. Someone may discover the falsified records. You, and your entire family could be asked to explain your actions. No, no, we cannot let your risk your reputations." She turned to Michael and grasped his hand. "Tell them that the risk is far too much."

5

*M*elissa stared out the window of her bedchamber. The snowfall that had kept them housebound on the duke's estate had finally ceased. Sherwyn's footmen had been able to travel this morning and had left at daybreak to fetch the archbishop. Even if the archbishop was forced to travel on horseback, Cayle and Becca had assured her that the man should arrive here by evening. Melissa was torn between a deep sadness that Frederick was dying and Freda would never know her true father, and abject relief that she and Michael could still be married.

A year of wearing the colors of mourning, black, grey, and mauves, would be bearable if she had Michael's support. Best of all, if the archbishop also married she and Michael, they wouldn't be forced by propriety to stay apart from each other while his family grieved. Though she was wracked with worries over anyone discovering their deceit over the dates of the two weddings. The scandal would rock all the families involved and Frederick's family would be shocked, and unlikely to welcome Melissa to their family, despite Freda being Frederick's biological child.

She groaned. Whichever way she looked at the situation, she was troubled. Michael, bless his kind heart, was convinced that Sherwyn's plan would work perfectly and that when the bridge was repaired and they could travel, everyone would accept her as his wife. And one thing that Michael had said stuck in her mind. They did love each other. She knew that the closeness they shared would last their lifetime. Knew deep inside that they were meant to be together, just as Michael believed.

Thankfully, Frederick seemed of a like mind, because if he'd objected to her relationship with Michael as he'd be entitled to do, she couldn't go through with the second part of their plan. Frederick was too gentlemanly to call her nasty names, but there would be others who would label her as a flirt and a woman with a fickle heart if they discovered that she'd married only minutes after her past lover had died. Marrying so quickly was nothing knew in their circles, because women were regarded as the weaker sex and therefore couldn't survive unless they were always under a man's protection. And having Michael's name would apparently, by Cayle and Richard's reasoning, keep she and her daughter safer than if she continued her fictitious life as a widow.

Many men saw widows as easy pickings and the men who had kidnapped Frederick all those years ago were apparently going to be even more desperate to rid themselves of anyone who could inherit Frederick's plantation. When she married Michael, her property would automatically become his to own, and manage, so that would eliminate she and Freda as targets, yet would heighten the threat to Michael.

A knock sounded on her door and she called, "Come in."

Michael stepped inside her room and closed the door behind him. "The archbishop is here. Sherwyn said we're ready to begin whenever you are."

She bit her lip. Standing before her was everything she'd ever envisioned for a wonderful future. A husband who would love and cherish her. A loving father for Freda, and for any other children they might be lucky enough to have together.

Michael walked towards her, but stopped an arm's length away. His fists were clenched at his sides, and the muscles around his jaw were pulled tight. "Are you having second thoughts about marrying me?"

"No, no, no." She took his hand and pulled him to her, sliding her arms under his coat and around his waist. She leant her head on his chest, listening to his strong and comforting heartbeat. "Not that." She looked up at him and smiled, trying to show him how much she loved him. "I'm simply feeling sad that Frederick has been with us, especially you, for such a short time."

"I know. I already miss him, despite not having him around for the past four years. We were as close as brothers for most of our lives, and he was my best friend." His chest heaved under her ear and she felt his hiccoughing breathing and knew he was fighting hard to keep his emotions under control for Frederick's sake, and hers.

Melissa let Michael lead her back to Frederick's bedchamber and guide her to stand close to Frederick, and opposite the man she was introduced to as the archbishop, and a distant relation of the duke's. Several other witnesses stood in a tight circle around the end of the bed, the women leaning into their husbands and other males for support. They held handkerchiefs to their faces, mopping at tears, but looking determined to carry through with this ceremony and put their considerable social support behind Melissa and Michael. She had no idea how she'd ever repay Becca, Laura, Charlotte, and the other women who had welcomed her to their family as if she was truly a sister to them, instead of the soon-to-be wife of their very distant cousin. That relationship thread was so thin as to be invisible, yet they'd promised each other that in the New Year the family records would be brought out, dusted off, and they'd trace back the St. Martin line and discover where their heredity path crossed with Michael's.

When the formalities of introductions and explanations of legal terms were explained, the archbishop spoke of the upcoming ceremony that would join Melissa with the shell of the man she'd taken as her lover for once brief night.

She sucked in a deep breath and took Frederick's hand in hers.

Someone loudly cleared his or her throat. They looked around.

Lady Charlotte Jamison shifted on her feet, looking embarrassed to have called attention to herself. She cleared her throat again, and Melissa noticed that she'd twisted the square of lined she held into a knot. A sense of foreboding washed over Melissa and her knees buckled. Luckily, Michael had hold of her arm and held her upright. She gave him a grateful smile before facing Charlotte again.

"What is it, Lottie?" Sherwyn asked his sister-in-law.

"I was helping to entertain the children earlier when you discussed this marriage, so I am assuming that this subject has already been discussed. Perhaps a solution to the problem already found?" She glanced between Cayle and Richard, her two protective brothers-in-law. "Correct me if I'm wrong, but doesn't our latest family law explicitly forbid a union between a man and his brother's widow?"

Brian, Sherwyn's brother, beamed at Charlotte as if she'd just solved the mysteries of the entire universe. Poor man, he clearly worshipped Charlotte, and no wonder. She was intelligent, extremely well-read, and a breathtaking beauty. Melissa might feel jealous if she didn't know that Charlotte was also one of the kindest women she'd ever encountered.

Sherwyn spoke first. "A good question, Lottie, and yes, one we've already discussed." He waved at his brother-in-law, Earl Winchester. "You understand Lord Lyndhurst's Marriage Act better than anyone. Perhaps you'd like to explain Michael's situation for everyone."

"You're quite correct, Lottie, that Michael couldn't marry Frederick's widow if he was Frederick's brother by blood, or to be as scientifically correct as Becca and Laura would prefer, consanguinity."

Frederick gave a humph, indicating his agreement. He'd also studied law and had kept abreast of new laws, and changed laws.

The earl dipped his head at Frederick. "Yes, Lyndhurst's new marriage laws would have been put in place not long before you were kidnapped. And thank goodness you thought of it this afternoon and brought it to our attention. Because yes, we all assumed that Michael was your brother by blood."

Michael nodded. "I called Frederick my brother from the start when I wen to live with his family after my parents were killed. I was a grieving and lonely child, so my wonderful aunt became my mother and I called her by that name until the day she died. In actual fact, I was her nephew and Frederick's cousin."

"And there is no legal reason why you cannot marry your cousin's widow. Europe's royal families are prime example of cousins marrying cousins. Blood cousins at that." He shrugged. "Even as Frederick's brother, you could do as many others are doing and ignore Lyndhurst's ridiculous law. Personally, I think it will be repealed before long. Too many people either object, or ignore the law."

Sherwyn thanked Richard and asked the archbishop to begin. Melissa remembered little of the service later, except that she held tightly to Frederick's hand and said 'I do' in all the correct places. In no time at all, she and Frederick were legally married and the arch-bishop took care of the paperwork.

Their witnesses said goodnight and left Melissa and Michael alone with Frederick. Melissa gratefully sank onto the chair that Michael brought forward for her. Frederick beckoned them both closer and Melissa and Michael and leaned closer to his face so he didn't have to strain to speak. He tried to lift his hand but the cere-mony had exhausted him. Melissa dabbed at her face with a hand-kerchief with one hand while grasping Frederick's trembling fingers in her other.

"You've made a dying man very happy." Frederick smiled, looking more content than he'd been all day. Melissa's face was awash with tears, and Michael wasn't much better. "I wish you both a lifetime of happiness."

Each sentence was punctuated by Frederick's harsh breathing, which sounded overly loud in the quiet room. There was no one in the room who wasn't tormented by Frederick's obvious pain each time his chest sucked in to his ribs in a move distressing to watch. "I know I don't have to ask the two of you to take good care of my daughter." Melissa's grip tightened on Michael's hand. They waited, breath held, while Frederick wheezed, in and out, until he'd inhaled enough air that he could speak again. "But I'd like to ask you to do something."

Melissa and Michael nodded in unison.

"Anything," Michael said, his voice hoarse. Melissa's was the same, due to the enormous lump blocking her throat.

"Would you tell Freda when she is older that her Uncle Frederick loved her very much."

"Her father," Melissa objected.

Frederick shook his head. "No, there is no point telling her that until she is much older, and capable of understanding. I'd be grateful if Freda thinks kindly of her deceased uncle."

"She will certainly know how much you loved her," Michael said.

"And," Frederick whispered, "do not ruin your own marriage by spending years mourning for me." Melissa shook her head in protest. "No, my dear, do this for me. Michael will make you a far netter husband than I would have if we'd married four years ago. Though I loved you, I was immature and arrogant. I know better now. It took chains and a ship's hull to remind me that a man should be grateful for the smaller things that we often take for granted. A home, food, family. They are the most important things."

Michael squeezed Melissa's waist. "Believe me, Frederick, I will thank the heavens for my good fortune every day that I have Melissa by my side as my wife. And our next child, if we are so blessed, will be named after you."

"Oh, yes," Melissa said. "Fredrick or Frederica Brandon. We promise that your name will continue."

Frederick squinted up at Melissa. "Tell me one more thing, did you use our family name, Brandon, so Freda would appear more legitimate?"

Beside her, Michael groaned. "I'm an idiot," he said. "You said our common name was because we must be related somewhere, back in time. It never occurred to me that you'd taken the name Brandon to be closer to the man you..."

"Loved," Melissa finished for him. "I did love you, Fredrick, and I wanted our daughter to have some connection to you. Though to be truthful, I hadn't thought my faux widowhood too carefully before the first person asked me the name of my deceased husband. I was so nervous that I blurted out your name, Frederick, without thinking. After that, it was too late to invent something else."

Fredrick smiled at her and Michael gave a snort of laughter before assuring her that, despite her lack of imagination in inventing her widow's name, they were both delighted that she already carried their name, meaning that little would need to be changed. Initial embroidered on handkerchiefs would be correct. Engravings on silver wedding gifts would be correct.

It took Melissa moment to realize that she was being teased, by her past lover and her new love. For the first time in hours, she smiled. Tentatively at first, but then with great relief. Everything would be all right after all. She considered herself the luckiest woman in the world to have met, and loved two such incredible men.

Melissa and Michael stayed with Frederick for another hour, during which Freda was brought to the room so her father could look at her pretty face while he could. When they left him, Melissa's heart was breaking, but there was nothing to be done except live their lives as Frederick wanted. Happily, and as a family.

6

The Duke of Sherwyn knocked on Melissa's door very early the next morning, his voice tight with suppressed emotion, and informed her that her husband, Lord Frederick Brandon had taken his last breath an hour earlier. Though she'd been awake all night waiting for this very news, she was overcome with grief and would have sunk to the floor if not for the support of Michael, who stood stoically behind Sherwyn.

Michael guided her to a seat and crouched in front of her. He held her hands when he explained how he'd sat with Frederick until he'd drawn the last breath of air into his fluid-filled lungs. Told her that his brother's passing had been peaceful and he was no longer in pain.

"I should have been there with him," Melissa protested.

"No, my love. He explicitly asked that you not be there to witness his final frailties. He wanted you to remember him as he was four years ago so that you could tell Freda that her uncle had been strong and healthy, not a man withering away with consumption."

Melissa nodded, while Michael continued to reassure her until she'd calmed and settled.

"The snow has stopped," Sherwyn said. "The bridge will be passable in another few days and you can both take Frederick's body home, where he wanted. His mother may no longer be alive, but she'll want her son buried next to her, I'm sure."

"Yes, that's exactly what she would want," Michael added. "At least I can keep my promise to bring her son home, even if it's not how any of us wanted to take him back there. And his father will be there. He'll want to bury his son in manner fitting to a Lord Brandon. Frederick has other family. They will be thankful to at least be able to grieve for their brother. Finally."

"Lady Brandon," Sherwyn said, making Melissa jump.

She put her hands to her face. "Oh, dear. I hadn't considered having a title. I've been plain Mrs. Brandon for so long that I'd forgotten about anything else. About Fredrick being a lord. And you." She waved a hand towards Michael. "I imagined your title was because you were Fredrick's brother."

"No, my parents held titles, so I came by mine in the usual way. Though I didn't use my title in the Orient and haven't become re-accustomed to it since I've been back in England."

Sherwyn snorted. "I had trouble becoming accustomed to mine after my father died. Being a duke is often a millstone around my neck. But at times like this, when I can influence family members, such as the archbishop, into doing what needs to be done with smudging church records, I am thankful that I have that sort of power." He grinned. "And Becca, my darling duchess, will never allow me to become an arrogant and useless type of duke. We're both pleased that we're able to assist you. You both deserve a lifetime of happiness." He shrugged. "if that means bending a few rules, so be it." He stood. "Now, we need to discuss our plans. It's time for a second marriage to be performed, if you're ready."

Melissa nodded and Michael helped her to her feet. "Come, my love. We should do this before the rest of the duke's visitors awaken. The less people aware of our hasty marriage the better."

The next few hours passed in a whirlwind for Michael and Melissa. They were now man and wife. Married at last, Michael thought, relieved that he could finally announce to the world that the woman he loved was his to love and protect forever. In a day or two, they would travel to his uncle's house. His home too. It seemed fitting that Frederick's daughter would be able to know her grandfather, her uncle, and her aunt. They'd welcome Melissa with open arms, and spoil Freda with treats and hugs, as every little girl should be indulged.

No one would know the details of the marriage between Melissa and Frederick, because the archbishop would inscribe the church record books in his usual scrawl, only this time his scrawl would appear more like a snail's trail across the parchment and even on the slim chance that anyone became suspicious, they'd not be able to read the dates. None of them.

When he and Melissa were finally alone, he took her hand and led her to the bed. No one would interrupt them this time and he could make love to his new wife all day long. Well perhaps not all day, as Freda would be looking for her mother soon, and for him. Freda had asked if she could called him papa, and his heart had swelled with so much love and pride that he'd thought it would burst out of his chest.

Melissa absently rubbed her stomach as she stretched back on the bed. He placed his hand over hers and circled her rounded abdomen with their entwined hands. "There is another reason I'm pleased we're already married. Do you know what it is?"

She lifted a hand and slid it around his neck, pulling him down to her. He knew what she wanted and he obliged with a long and inciting kiss, long enough that she sighed into his mouth and touched her tongue to his. He also knew that she was doing this deliberately to distract him.

"When were you planning on telling me?" He felt her startle, before she gave him a little laugh. "You know?"

"Of course I know. How could I not when we've been as close, as intimate, as two beings can be for several months. I know your body intimately, know it netter than my own." He placed a hand over her stomach. "You've missed your monthly inconvenience for the last two months." He touched his lips to one breast, sucking through the material until the fabric became damp and he could feel her aroused nipple under his tongue. "And not that I'm complaining, but your breasts are larger than before. Both Sherwyn and the earl have told me that it's a delightful side benefit of having a pregnant wife."

She chuckled. "A side benefit?"

He grinned. "A delightful one."

"But Michael, how will we explain our child's early arrival into the world?"

"Ah, but we have the St. Martin and the Jamison families to help us. They will ensure that the Ton believes that we've been married for quite a long time. Therefore, our daughter will be born well within the allotted nine months. See, no gossip. Problem solved."

She smiled. "I'm positive that our *son* will appreciate a scandal free arrival into our family."

As he removed Melissa's clothing, Michael took time to kiss each bare patch of skin. He laved it with his tongue and blew air onto the area, causing Melissa to moan and wriggle and arch up into his eager mouth. He swallowed, hard. He didn't deserve this amazing woman but he was going to spend the rest of his life proving that he was the right husband for her, and the perfect father for their children.

"I love you," he murmured next to her ear, sweeping the shell with his tongue and feeling her full body shiver.

"I love you too," she said, groaning again as he nibbled her neck.

"And, there will be no scandal attached to our name. Because if Cayle and Becca tracked a madwoman and had her sent to jail and still avoided scandal, and if Richard and Laura survived several attempts on their lives and yet side-stepped all hint of scandal, then we, you and I, two supremely intelligent, experienced, and well-suited individuals will obviously be able to avoid any hint of a December scandal."

Melissa threw back her head and laughed. "I adore you, Michael Brandon. And I adore all your crazy friends."

He grinned. "Good, because they all want to celebrate Christmas with us next year. Sherwyn has decided that December is not the best time of year to retreat to the country. Too much snow. Too many uninvited guests." He tickled her until she squealed. "Though if they intend staying with us, I shall have better door locks installed, because I want more alone time with my beautiful wife and my lovely daughters."

"Daughter and son," she corrected. He let her have the last word, knowing she'd not be speaking too much after that as he had much better uses for her delectable mouth than talking.

EXCERPT EMBRACING SCANDAL

Martin House, Mayfair, London, 1843

Curse the city and its constant interferences. Secluded in his fire-heated library, Cayle St. Martin, Duke of Sherwyn, attempted to block out all things British by imagining himself back on a Mediterranean beach, unfettered, unhurried, and warm.

The brandies he'd downed didn't guarantee peacefulness but they fired his blood and ensured a few hours of deeper sleep. No doubt they, and several glasses of wine at the ball, would also earn him a pounding head in the morning as well. His butler's shoes echoed on the marble tiles in the hall, the reverberations making it easy to trace Jenner's progress to and from the front portico as he opened, closed and secured the heavy oak doors, twice.

At the first knock on his front door, Cayle had listened and dismissed the disturbance as inconsequential. After the second knock, a long silence had been shattered by solitary footsteps as the butler strode towards the library where Cayle sat, comfortably sprawled in an overstuffed armchair.

Despite now living in theoretically peaceful England and not having heard a stranger's tread, old habits of mistrust died hard.

Cayle eased up his trouser leg and gripped the hilt of his thin bladed knife, an assurance in case his butler wasn't alone.

Jenner tapped and pushed the door open. "Your Grace."

"Yes, Jenner." Cayle relaxed his grip on the knife and sighed. He flicked his tongue around the rim of the crystal goblet, savoring the last drops of brandy. If only his new ducal status, with its never-ending demands on his time, was as palatable as his late father's well-aged liquor. "Who was at the door?"

Displaying his habitual unruffled demeanor, his butler crossed the library and deftly plucked the glass from Cayle's lax fingers before he dropped it onto his stepmother's latest extravagance, a thick Persian carpet.

"A person who demanded an audience with the Duke of Sherwyn." His butler's nose raised another notch, a seemingly impossible feat, as he placed the brandy glass on his silver tray without even the tiniest clink. "The individual was informed that His Grace was not at home."

Cayle rubbed a hand over his tired eyes. On occasion, Jenner's puffed-up snobbishness drove Cayle mad. Yet when he wanted to be left alone, Jenner's inflexible stance at the front door was a blessing. His butler could sniff out beggars and pretenders at a hundred yards and only the highest-ranking members of the ton were invited inside these hallowed halls. If the St. Martin's lofty address failed to deter unwanted visitors, Jenner's haughty manner generally succeeded.

"Did he say why he wished to see me at this ungodly hour?"

"No, Your Grace, <u>she</u> did not enlighten me."

"She?" His feet hit the floor. "What sort of woman comes knocking on doors at this hour?" He studied his butler's stern expression. "Obviously not any of the ladies of my acquaintance."

"From her shabby attire and her insistent manner, I deduced that she was in dire need of employment. Either as a maid, in which case I advised she present herself to the housekeeper at the tradesman's entrance later in the morning, or by attracting a richer patron than her present keeper. As her appearance would offend the sensibilities of any Mayfair gentleman, such as yourself, I insisted that she immediately remove herself from Your Grace's doorstep or I would summon the watch."

"Ah, well done, Jenner," Cayle said. He hid his grin as he pushed himself to his feet with the assistance of the wide chair arms. "So, if our first visitor was so easily disposed of, who knocked the second time?"

"Of that, Your Grace, I am uncertain. The street was empty apart from a street urchin running along the pavement. I assumed the boy had knocked on our door as a prank."

Cayle strolled to the doorway and stared down the dimly lit passageway. Nothing moved. He couldn't detect any sound apart from the final sputtering of the last candles burning out.

"Most likely some boyish lark. A dare." Yet the hairs on the back of his neck stood to attention. "Though I don't doubt your capabilities, Jenner, I shall recheck the locks before I retire. It's long past time we were both in our beds."

Jenner dipped a small, stiff nod. "Indeed, Your Grace."

Cayle had privately spent three grueling months untangling the family's finances while publicly pretending to be one of his peers, lazy and without direction or ambition. But even now he had no inkling as to how Jenner regarded him. As the black sheep who'd been booted out by his father after an incident at a ball. Or the heir who'd not returned in time to stop his father send the family close to ruin when his wits became addled.

He hoped perhaps their old retainer had forgiven him and they could return to a more acceptable relationship. Though Jenner's bending spine appeared to be from a bone-deep weariness, the equivalent of Cayle's own exhaustion, rather than forgiveness of past sins.

Jenner walked with his measured steps towards the servants' quarters. He stopped halfway down the hallway and turned back. "One hesitates to speak out of turn, Your Grace, but you appear to be suffering from more than an excess of brandy and overwork this evening. Before your time abroad, your disposition was generally regarded as steady and cheerful. However, your recent somberness has been noted by the staff."

Cayle froze at such candid observations from his reserved butler. According to his stepmother, fraternizing with underlings was a sin as horrifying as dressing oneself without a valet's assistance.

Jenner spoke quietly yet his words resonated down the tomb-like passageway. "The staff has asked me to thank you, Your Grace, for working so tirelessly to restore the household and the estates to their former glory. They ... All of us, pray that Your Grace will resolve the family's difficulties quickly. Once the reputation of the St. Martin name has been re-established, we hope you may find time, once again, to see to your own happiness."

Household servants knew everything that happened and often before the inhabitants became aware of events. So it came as no surprise that the coldness between Cayle and his stepmother had been discussed below stairs. His brothers regarded Julia as Satan reincarnate and she'd certainly helped ignite the feud between Cayle and his father that had seen him dispatched to the Continent, out of sight and out of everyone's mind.

Since his return, he and Julia had made a pact. An agreement that he hoped would see her out of their lives once and for all. But she was determined to see her title of Duchess of Sherwyn returned to its, and her, former glory before she'd remove her talons from his hide. Being chained to her side on public occasions was sending him further into hell.

His brandy-mellowed mind could easily envision her so-called friends, the pretend elite of London's society, being the ones to pound on his door. Each time he attended a societal event with Julia clinging to his arm he was reminded of his responsibilities to the St. Martin name and what he owed his brothers. Julia sent ladies to his side at these events. Whispered in their ears the long list of his titles. Dangled him in front of their lemon-bleached noses like a carrot to be awarded to the greediest and grasping donkey.

Julia believed herself subtle and congratulated herself on selecting a ready-to-breed duchess who would be under her command. Under normal circumstances, Cayle would respond to these fast ladies with their none-too-subtle sexual advances with a few seductive moves. Stolen kisses at a ball that might, or might not, lead to a few pleasurable romps in the lady's bed.

He regarded his self-enforced celibacy as a temporary inconvenience, nothing more. But his stressful months were not only tormenting him mentally. His ignored physical needs had started clamoring for more attention. Solitary relief was too brief to truly satisfy him.

He missed the feel of a woman's soft body wrapped around him, and each time those women brushed his body, accidentally or on purpose, he imagined arranging an assignation. They'd meet in the conservatory. He'd lift the woman's satin skirts, push aside the layers of petticoats, and plunge, without ceremony, into her sweet body.

Then sanity would return. Julia's hawkish eyes followed every move he made as she waited for him to make another stupid mistake. To drop his guard and find himself trapped by another woman in a compromising situation. To secure his brothers' futures, he needed to stick to his plan. That plan included avoiding women; all women.

Jenner cleared his throat. "And as an older man, might I also be so bold as to suggest that solutions to a gentleman's troubles often present themselves after a good night's sleep and without a sick head and heaving stomach."

In the half-dark, Cayle grunted his agreement.

"Apart from which," Jenner's voice rose a notch, "mindless swilling of your father's perfectly aged brandy is a gross injustice."

Jenner left and Cayle slumped against the wall. His battles with both the accounting ledgers and his ghastly stepmother must be disconcerting his staff, if his lofty butler had lowered himself to dispensing fatherly advice. He started towards the street door, instinctively walking close to the wall and avoided the open middle path. His senses warned him of another presence, mystical or physical. As he'd made peace with the house's resident ghost when still a boy, the likely explanation was a material presence. Well, then! He dealt with physical combat better than emotional or physic stresses.

With fluid movements, he retrieved his knife, slipped past the portico doors, and edged towards the medieval laird's chair. From the dark corner came the scent of flowers, faint yet appreciable. A small shape huddled in the depth of the chair, half-concealed by the wooden arms and with scuffed boots hanging at least a foot above the floor. His uninvited visitor must be either a woman or a young lad.

His nostrils filled with flowery scents and reminded him of happier times when bouquets were picked in meadows and tied with ribbons and love. Definitely a female and one possessed of enough coin to be wearing a tantalizing and expensive fragrance. Memories stirred but he pushed them aside. Pleasurable recollections didn't belong here, in his cold hallway on this miserable night.

He peered at the chair. An old coat engulfed an undersized frame and a soft brimmed hat dipped over her face. He lowered his blade and rested the steel's tip against his thigh.

"You can come out now. We're alone."

Quiet, even breaths purred from the stationary figure. He frowned. Ridiculous idea that any she-thief would sneak into his house and fall asleep in the entrance. He bent closer. Without warning, she sucked in a breath so deep it hissed like a blacksmith's iron sizzling in water.

He jumped back and every muscle clamped like a vise as his error, his own greenhorn foolishness, registered like a slap in the face. She was awake.

"Stand up." He raised his knife and waved it in a circle between them. "Let me see the person audacious enough to break into my house."

Taking her time, she slid off the chair and stood. The cloak, more decrepit than any respectable housemaid would wear, fell into soggy folds over her skirt. A damp dark veil drooped over the hat's brim, while from beneath the hat, bright auburn hair tumbled like a waterfall to her shoulders and wet strands clung to her cheeks. He reached out to lift her veil but she leapt back, skittish as a new foal, and banged the backs of her legs against the chair.

"I won't harm you if you behave."

Silence.

As a sign of trust between them, he lowered the knife. "But I am intrigued. Many people try to slip past my butler. Before you, they've always failed. You've obviously had a lot of practice at entering houses illegally."

No comment.

"You must be an excellent thief."

Her hands clenched at her sides. Her cloak was pushed aside when she planted her fists on her hips. "I. Am. Not. A. Thief."

Though he'd finally goaded her into speaking, her indignation barely registered. His eye was drawn to the feminine form she'd unwittingly exposed when the thin fabric of her skirt pulled tight across her stomach.

"If you're not here to steal, why go to such lengths to get inside my house."

"I needed to see you." She flicked clumps of wet hair over her shoulders. "Alone."

"And I would definitely like to see more of you."

For a second time, he tried to lift her veil. She flinched. He waited. Frustration rose as he pondered her need for obscurity. Was she a ruthless robber avoiding detection? A harlot trying to appear exotic and mysterious? Or worse, a husband-hunting miss pretending coyness to ambush a duke.

He let his eyes drift upwards from an ill-fitting brown skirt to hover where her full breasts strained against bodice fabric thinned with age and moisture. After a long appreciative look, his gaze meandered up and over those never-ending cascades of bright-colored hair.

His scrutiny might unnerve many women but this mysterious female merely huffed, stiffened her spine, and waited. Her breathing sounded louder, a little faster, yet she stood squarely and anchored her gaze around his upper chest. And took the offensive.

"I'm relieved you discovered my face at last. I was beginning to think I'd need to draw you a map."

He treated her to his most roguish and unrepentant grin. "Ah, but you see, my sweet, if you haven't come here to rob me--"

"Don't be ridiculous."

"Then, you're a puzzle. If you were better dressed, I'd assume you'd come to entertain me." He stared at her sodden and shapeless cloak and dull clothing. "Ladybirds tend to dress like peacocks. Even my maids dress better than you. And though I approve of what's on display--"

He nodded towards her chest, where her breasts squeezed up and over her ill-fitting bodice like fruit spilling from a basket. She glanced down and gasped. She tugged the bodice's folds together but managed a mere thumb's breadth. That garment obviously belonged to someone far less endowed.

"Your speech is far too refined for any street walker." He tapped a finger to his mouth. "Did my well-meaning brothers send you?"

A crease dipped between narrow brows the same hue as her hair, reddish-brown but leaning more towards red, and the coloring blend he'd always preferred.

"Your brothers?" Noticing that his eyes were roaming over her body again, she huffed and tried to tug her bodice upwards. "I wish you'd stop speaking in riddles. You're making my head spin."

With reluctance, he lifted his attention back to her face. "I thought they might have sent you to cheer me up. Consolation for my fortitude in dealing with all this." He waved his hand to indicate his house.

"Nonsense. You were trained from birth to take charge of all this."

Another moment of déja vu tugged at his mind. He ignored the off-putting and ill-fitting garments and tried to make out the female beneath.

His door knocker clanged for the third time.

"Bloody hell! Can I never have peace?"

He spun towards the door, eager to reach it before the knocker echoed a fourth time. Before it woke every servant in his household. Or worse. Before it roused the Dowager Duchess of Sherwyn, who'd retired an hour ago to her own expansive wing.

"No. Wait."

His still unidentified female ran behind him. She clutched the sleeve of his right arm, the one dangling his knife. As one, they looked down at the blade swinging beside his thigh. She made no sounds of terror. Nor did she recoil or tremble. He was struggling to sort out this female paradox when she tightened her grip on his arm.

"Don't open the door. Please."

"I must or they'll knock again and awaken my servants."

She clung like a limpet. "Please, I beg of you. Send them away. Don't give me up."

"Them? Who's after you? The watch?"

"I've broken no laws. Do as I ask, please. For your own safety."

He frowned at her in the dull light, trying to see past the hat and the endless hair to the woman beneath, to understand what she thought. What she plotted.

"Very well. But in return, you'll reveal yourself and explain why you're here. Agreed?"

The ugly hat bobbed twice, before she disappeared back into the shadowy corner. He opened the door, knife grip tightened, to confront the two men who stood in the rain wearing sodden coats and sheltering under black umbrellas.

ABOUT THE AUTHOR

Tag Line - Making history fun, one year at a time.

I now live in a sunny part of Australia after spending many years in developing countries in the South Pacific. I love traveling, anywhere and everywhere, meeting crazy characters, and visiting the Australian outback.

My sexy heroes and feisty heroines challenge tradition, and though they might live a privileged life, they also understand the seamier parts of life.

I can be found in many Facebook groups talking about books and history and am always busy on Twitter, Instagram, and my personal favorite, Pinterest.

To learn more about Suzi Love and my new releases, join my newsletter at my suzilove.com. I am on Instagram and Goodreads and have lots of Pinterest Boards as suziloveoz. And please join my Facebook Group, Suzi Love's Lovelies, to keep up with my news on books and history.

Please visit my WEBSITE

Email me: suzi@suzilove.com

BOOKS BY SUZI LOVE

Fiction By Suzi Love

Embracing Scandal Book 1 Scandalous Siblings Series

Scenting Scandal Book 2 Scandalous Siblings Series

December Scandal Book 3 Scandalous Siblings Series

The Viscount's Pleasure House Book 1 Irresistible Aristocrats

Four Times A Virgin Book 2 Irresistible Aristocrats

Pleasure House Ball Book 3 Irresistible Aristocrats

Petunia and the Pearl Diver Book 4 Irresistible Aristocrats

Loving Lady Katharine Book 5 Irresistible Aristocrats

Love After Waterloo

Kelly's Justice

Outback Arrival

Old Sydney Town

Non-Fiction By Suzi Love

History Of Christmases Past Book 1 History Events

Easter In Images Book 2 History Events

History of Valentine's Day

Regency Overview Book 1 Regency Life Series

Young Gentleman's Day Book 2 Regency Life Series

Older Gentleman's Day Book 3 Regency Life Series

Young Lady's Day Book 4 Regency Life Series

Older Lady's Day Book 5 Regency Life Series

Self Publishing: Absolute Beginners Guide.

HISTORY NOTES SERIES

Here are some of the many titles in this Non-Fiction History Series.

Coming Soon:-

History Notes Underwear
History Notes Grand Tour
History Notes Mail Deliveries
History Notes Peerage
History Notes Food
History Notes Carriages
History Notes Money
History Notes Sewing
History Notes Hats
History Notes Mourning
History Notes Furniture
History Notes Shoes
History Notes Trades
History Notes Clubs
History Notes Fans
History Notes Sports

Historic London

Overview
Bridges
Hospitals
Churches
Famous

REVIEWS

Reviews are like gold to authors. I would appreciate it if you could leave a review, good or bad, for this book at any book retailer.

And don't forget, to get insider news about my book releases, any discounted books or contests that I am a part of, you should sign up for my newsletter. I promise you will only ever hear from me when I have exciting news, about me or my other author friends. www.-suzilove.com

You can send me an email : suzi@suzilove.com.

Or send a letter : Suzi Love, 258/ 52 University Way, Sippy Downs, Queensland, 4556, Australia.

www.ingramcontent.com/pod-product-compliance
Lightning Source LLC
Chambersburg PA
CBHW071314200626
46813CB00015B/2188